Blood TIES

MAYHEM MAKERS

LA FAMIGLIA DE LUCA BOOK THREE

USA TODAY BESTSELLING AUTHOR
KRISTINE ALLEN

Blood Ties, 1st Edition Copyright 2023 by Kristine Allen, Demented Sons Publishing, LLC.
All Rights Reserved.

Published in the United States of America. First published May 15, 2023.
Cover Design: Clarise Tan, CT Cover Creations
Photographer: Reggie Deanching
Cover Model: Cody Smith; image licensed for use by R+M Photography
Editing: Shelby Limón, Bookworm Edits & Creations, LLC.

Paperback ISBN-13: 978-1-953318-13-8

The purchase of this e-book, or book, allows you one legal copy for your own personal reading enjoyment on your personal computer or device. This does not include the right to resell, distribute, print or transfer this book, in whole or in part to anyone, in any format, via methods either currently known or yet to be invented, or upload to a file sharing peer to peer program, except in the case of brief quotations embodied in critical reviews and certain other noncommercial uses. It may not be re-sold or given away to other people. Such action is illegal and in violation of the U.S. Copyright Law. Criminal copyright infringement, including infringement without monetary gain, is investigated by the FBI and is punishable by up to 5 years in federal prison and a fine of $250,000 (http://www.fbi.gov/ipr/). Thank you for respecting the hard work of this author.

This is a work of fiction. Names, characters, businesses, places, events, and incidents are either the product of the author's imagination or used in a fictitious manner. Any resemblance to actual persons, living or dead, or actual events is purely coincidental. The publisher does not have any control and does not assume any responsibility for author or third-party websites or their content. For information, contact the author at kristine.allen.author@gmail.com. Thank you for supporting this author and her rights.

Warning: This book may contain offensive language, explicit violence, adult and explicit sexual situations. Mature audiences only, 18+ years of age.

Alessio De Luca…

Once upon a time, there was a young man who ran away for a chance at a different life. Then I f*cked up and went back. Turns out I like the darkness too much.

But now that darkness haunts me.

As the notorious hit man, The Huntsman, I kill without remorse. Feelings are not an option. After all, my family's legacy taught me that the world is cold—and now, so am I.

Until I have her in my sights and I can't pull the trigger.

Like a fool, I went and fell for her. Now The Huntsman has become the hunted and I have to keep her safe from the killers on our tail.

A poisonous cauldron of lies is drowning us, and no one is who they seem. My family is poised on the brink of war and I'm a target because of my last name.

She needs to trust me. But if she finds out I was supposed to kill her, I'll lose her. Not happening.

I'll find a way. Because I. Never. Back. Down.

I finally finished this book during Nurses Week, so it seemed fitting that this one be for you—the nurses of the world. We rock!

Blood TIES

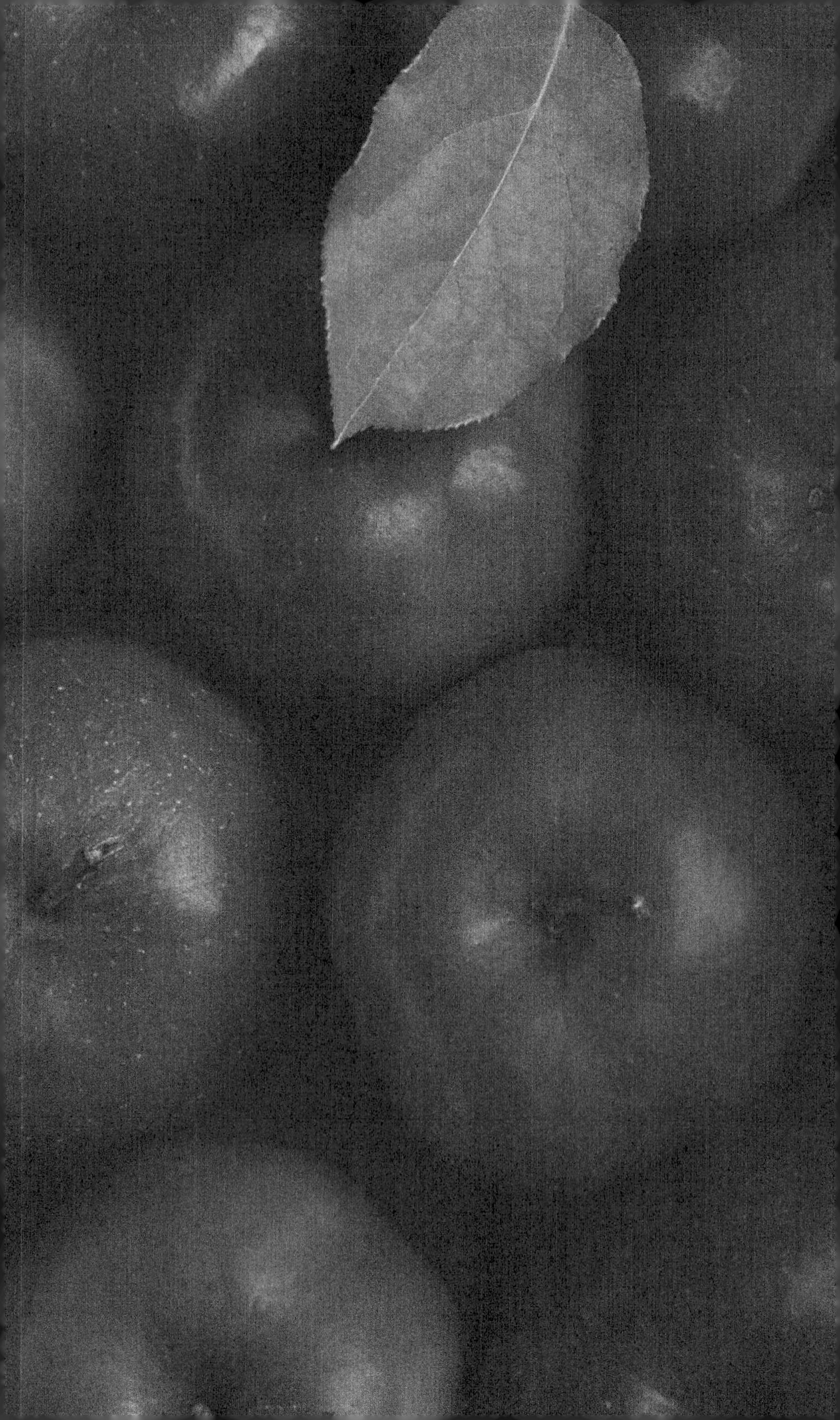

PROLOGUE

Jade

As I stared in the mirror, I smoothed a finger over my brow and wondered if it was time for more Botox. Maybe I might schedule a little plastic surgery to tighten up my jawline. In the background, my husband and his personal assistant, Carl, were discussing his schedule for the week. For the most part, I tuned them out.

Until I heard something that made my lip curl.

"Your daughter is so beautiful. I don't think I've ever seen someone so stunning, and goodness, she looks just like you. It's so fortunate that she found you," Carl said. Little kiss-ass.

"I just wish I'd known about her sooner. I feel like I missed so much. After being unable to have children all these years, I had no idea I could've fathered a child. But I have her now, and I don't plan to waste a day. You have my luncheon with her scheduled in, correct? I'm not missing that," Justin insisted.

I rolled my eyes. Little did he know, I made sure I couldn't have children. Who the hell wanted stretch marks and a torn vagina? Then, screaming children to deal with all the time? Ugh, no, thank you. Little soul-suckers, if you asked me. Besides, why would I want to share my husband's money with some spoiled little brat? I hadn't been with him for five years for nothing.

"Of course not. I have the time blocked off," Carl oozed.

"Excellent. I'm heading out for my meeting with the people from Denizen to discuss the merger. Hold my calls. Knowing them, it's going to be a late night," Justin announced before I heard his approach.

"Jade, I'm leaving. Are you sure you don't want to come with?" Justin asked me before he leaned over and brushed his lips on my forehead.

"No, darling, I'd be bored to tears, but thank you," I cooed. "Be careful. I don't like that news you got."

Justin gave me that soft smile that he reserved for me. He slipped a hand into the deep neckline of my silk robe and cupped one of my tits he'd paid for. "I'll be fine. She assured me that not all premonitions are set in stone. Wait up for me?" he murmured as his dark hair fell over his forehead.

"Of course," I told him with a sultry curve of my red lips. At least Justin had stayed in shape, and the sex was amazing.

"Damn, I wish I hadn't agreed to meet them for drinks tonight."

"This deal is important to you. You know they like to discuss business over dinner and drinks when they're here. Things are looking good with them, right?"

"It is. Hopefully, we'll come to a mutually satisfying agreement soon. Then we'll hand it over to the attorneys to finish up. I'll be home as soon as I can, baby," he promised, then gave me a kiss and a playful wink.

He left, and I resumed my study in the mirror.

"Jade, I got those emails sent that you asked me to take care of," Carl simpered behind me.

Taking a deep breath, I pasted a smile on my face and slowly spun on my stool to face him. "Excellent. And is everything else in place?"

"Yes, Jade."

I stood up and ran my fingers along the edge of the robe. Carl's eyes zeroed in on the movement. He stepped closer. "Are you sure we're doing the right—"

"Carl, it's the only way. We've discussed this. You don't know the things he has forced me to endure. He's not the same person everyone else sees, not when we're alone. I can't live like this anymore. With his money and the prenuptial agreement, he would leave me destitute and paint me out to be a terrible person." I gave him my most pitiful stare. The tear and the quivering bottom lip should've gotten me an Oscar.

If I'd had a better agent, I could've had parts that made me famous. Instead, I had small parts in a few big movies and starred in several low-budget films. When I'd met Justin at an after party, I'd seen my golden ticket and walked away from Hollywood.

Carl quickly closed the distance and took my hands in his. "I'll never hurt you. You know that, right? I love you with every fiber of my being."

I ran my hand over his balding head and leaned down slightly to feather my lips over his cheek. "I know. I love you too, and I'm so very grateful for you. This is the perfect time. He believes everything that stupid psychic says, and she told him he was going to die. Everything is playing out in our favor.

When it's done, we will have the financial security to start over somewhere new. Don't you want to be with me forever?"

"Oh, Jade, you know I do," he assured me with a lovesick stare.

My lips lifted in a relieved smile as I gazed at him like he was my hero. Then I cradled his sagging jowls and kissed him with a passion I sure as shit didn't feel.

He began to grope me over the deep green silk before his fumbling hands unfastened the tie on my robe and he pushed it over my shoulders. I made the appropriate moans and groans before we moved to the bed. His slobbering attempts at foreplay had me cringing inside.

As I faked the best orgasm of my life, I dug my nails convincingly into Carl's thin back.

"I love you, I love you, I love you," he chanted as he finished.

I'm counting on that. Then I only have two more steps and I'll be living in the lap of luxury for the rest of my life.

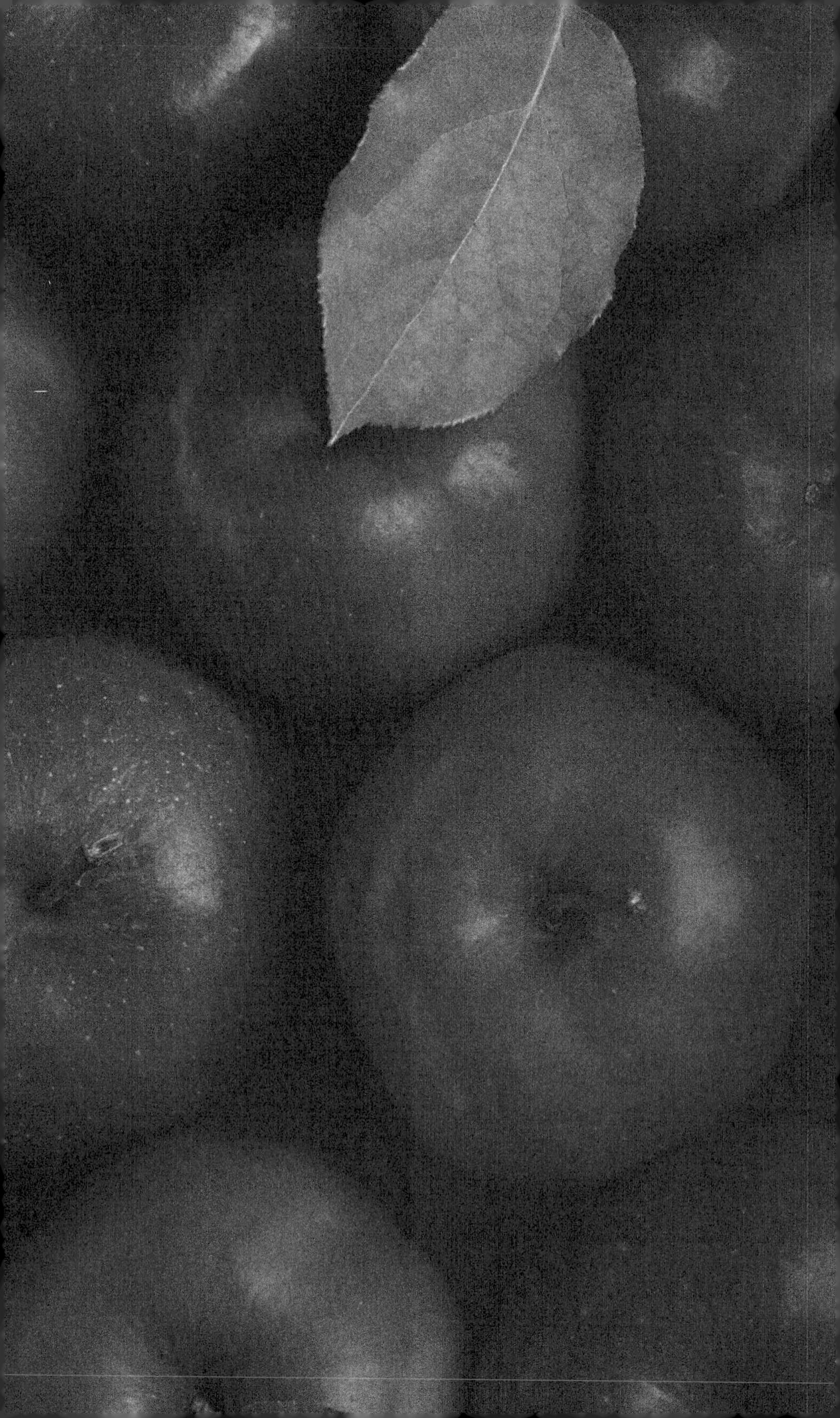

Chapter ONE

Nivea

"NUMB LITTLE BUG"—EM BEIHOLD

The first clod of dirt hit the casket and I jumped. When I looked around, I wondered how many people saw me do that. When I did, I made eye contact with my biological father's wife, Jade. The coldness in her eyes sent a shiver down my spine worse than the icy wind that cut to my bones. Her blood-red lips made a slight curl of derision and I frowned.

I'd never done anything to the woman and yet I could tell she hated me. Maybe it was because over the last year since I'd found my biological father, we'd become close and spent a lot of time together. She seemed selfish of his time and usually pouted when we did something she didn't want to do. In the end, we did most things without her.

Now he was dead.

This wasn't fair.

I'd only just found him.

Considering I'd lived the majority of my life not knowing who either of my biological parents were, I shouldn't be this attached so quickly. Should I? Was that normal? I had no idea. I'd never really felt "normal" anyway.

What I did feel was heartbroken. We should've had so many more years together. He was so young. Only forty-seven. From what he and I had pieced together, my mother had been young, and they had a brief affair. I think that was code for one-night stand, because he said he wasn't exactly sure who she was. He'd been engaged to his first wife, and my mother hadn't wanted a kid, so up for adoption I went.

Don't get me wrong, I had no complaints about my life. My adoptive parents were good to me and I loved them. They were open and believed I had a right to know I was adopted. Mom and Dad always said I was extra loved because they wanted me so much. They'd offered to come with me today, but I hadn't thought it was right. Now I wished they were here.

People started offering Jade condolences and her expression immediately morphed to one of utter devastation. Truthfully, this funeral was all for her benefit. Justin had been cremated. The coffin they buried contained his urn—to fulfill his wishes. He hadn't wanted the coffin—that was all Jade.

"We're so sorry for your loss."

"He was such a good man."

"He will be greatly missed."

They went on and on, but no one said anything to me. That was my cue to leave. With the black layers of my dress blowing in the bitter wind, I walked over the snow-crusted, uneven ground toward the road where I had parked with the rest of the cars.

A profound sadness hit me as I opened the door of my Porsche Macan, and I cast one last glance back.

Jade gave me another glare. Then she dissolved into tears, and Justin's personal assistant pulled out a handkerchief for her.

Heart heavy, I got in and started my car, then I drove away. It seemed so final. Oh, who was I kidding? It was. He was gone.

Tears fell the whole way home.

I drove back to my loft condo, parked in the parking garage across the street. Wrapping my scarf around my neck, I made sure it covered my nose. I pulled my coat tighter around my body and trudged up to my place.

Still sniffling, I changed into an old T-shirt and a baggie pair of bib-overalls. Then I used a bandana to pull back my jet-black hair. I opened the massive industrial windows and let the cold air hit me. I needed the rush of fresh air and I'd soon be sweating so I'd appreciate the cool breeze.

With a sad scan, I wished it was spring and I was watering all my flowers I normally had on the oversized ledges outside.

For a few moments, I stood there. Eyes closed and face to the sun, I let it shine its weak rays on me as I ran through the last year and the time I'd been able to spend with Justin— my biological father. In my mind, I heard the sound of birds carried through the air as they twittered and landed in one of my flower beds before they took off again.

Though I knew it wasn't real, it comforted me to know that spring would eventually arrive and with it, new life.

My phone rang, making me open my eyes, and I went looking for it. It was on my bed with my clothes and my purse. A smile lit my face at the caller. I didn't know how she always knew I needed to hear her voice.

"Hi, Mom."

"Hi, baby. Are you okay?"

As I sat on the edge of the mattress, my eyes caught on the small framed photo of me and Justin. I kept it near the larger one of me and my parents. Side by side, the similarities between us were uncanny—same bright blue eyes, same midnight black hair, same smile. I sighed. "Yes, and no. Does that even make sense?"

"Of course it does. He was a part of you, and I think you'd grown to love him. It would be an extremely emotional time for anyone with a heart."

A flash of my "stepmother" went through my mind. I snorted. "Yeah, everyone except his wife. I still don't know why he was married to her."

My mom laughed. "Oh, I'm sure you do. She was very beautiful, and he was in the spotlight often. She looked good on his arm and I'm sure he was very much in love with her."

I wasn't so sure about that, but I kept my opinion to myself. My mom was a good-hearted person who always looked for the best in everyone. Not a terrible trait to have, but she did tend to be a bit naïve at times. Probably why my dad was always very in-tuned to her "projects." He was good at ensuring she wasn't taken advantage of.

"And I'm sure the sex was good!" Dad called out from the background.

"Dad!" I blurted out, though I shouldn't be shocked at all that he'd said that. My dad was very open. Very, um, blunt. I wanted to laugh.

"Honey!" Mom chided.

"Okay, I'm sure he was probably very in love with her," he conceded from near the phone. Then he hollered into the phone. "Nivea, we love you! You say the word and we'll be on a plane to be with you!"

My lips quirked. "Thanks, Dad."

I'd been blessed. My adoptive parents were amazing and my biological father, Justin, had been too. My biological mother? Who knew. She made her part of the adoption process so airtight that I couldn't find her.

Justin, on the other hand, hadn't known about me at all. He said that was a rough time in his life. He'd been engaged to his first wife and didn't want to get married. It was a marriage that his family had pushed for but held no emotional bond for him or her. Their marriage had ended up lasting less than three years.

After that, he really went wild and sowed a lot of oats. He'd returned to his manwhore ways—his words, not mine.

We found out my bio-mom had forged his signature for the adoption and made sure her info was never released. Great genes on that side.

"Well, you let me know if you change your mind. We're always here for you, Niv." Mom was the best.

"I appreciate you guys so much. Thanks for being awesome."

"Anytime, baby girl, anytime," she assured.

We wrapped up our call and I stuck my phone in my back pocket. A shiver shook me from the open windows telling me it was time to get busy. Then I went back to my work area. I set my favorite playlist and turned the volume up to be heard over my equipment. I thanked the good Lord for the soundproofing my parents had paid for so I didn't make enemies of my neighbors below me.

A quick inventory told me I had what I needed. I grabbed the helmet and my welder, then finished constructing the steel frame. Next came the foam core that I sealed with latex. Finally, I began working with the heated clay.

Deep in the zone, I lost myself in the warm clay as I made the rough form. I meticulously carved out the details of the fairy's four-foot wings. I'd already finished the majority of the sections, and the wings were the last pieces. When I was done, and all the sections were welded together, she'd be a bronze statue that was destined for outside a children's museum in Texas.

So far, I was way ahead of schedule.

Which was good because I had plenty more commissions lined up.

Before I knew it, it was getting dark, and I glanced up in surprise. I'd been so absorbed in my work that I'd completely lost track of time. My stomach growled, reminding me that I hadn't eaten since my bagel at breakfast.

"Shit. I gotta stop doing that," I muttered. Despite the cold air coming in through the windows all day, I was soaked in sweat. Now that I'd quit moving, the chill was setting in.

After washing my hands, I made a peanut butter

sandwich. Munching on it, I went around the loft closing the windows. I was humming along to a Lana Del Ray song as I moved. When I got to the side that faced the top floor of a parking garage, I got a chill. I paused, sandwich half in my mouth, processing the strange feeling.

Was that the glow of a cigarette in the corner where one of the lights was burned out?

No sooner had I questioned it, then I saw it go out.

Shaking off the eerie feeling of being watched, I closed the window. Then I went to the corner, worked the cords to close the drapes on that side of the condo. I'd never been nervous in my home. I loved it. It was the top floor of an old building down in the River North neighborhood in downtown Chicago.

When my parents bought it for me for my graduation from SAIC—School of the Art Institute of Chicago—it was four apartments. They had the entire floor gutted and remodeled, so I had a huge studio area and then an open-concept condo that appealed to my artist's heart. I hated feeling confined. Yeah, I knew I was spoiled as fuck, but I can promise I appreciated it.

Still, I couldn't shake the chills, and I did something out of character for me.

I closed all the curtains.

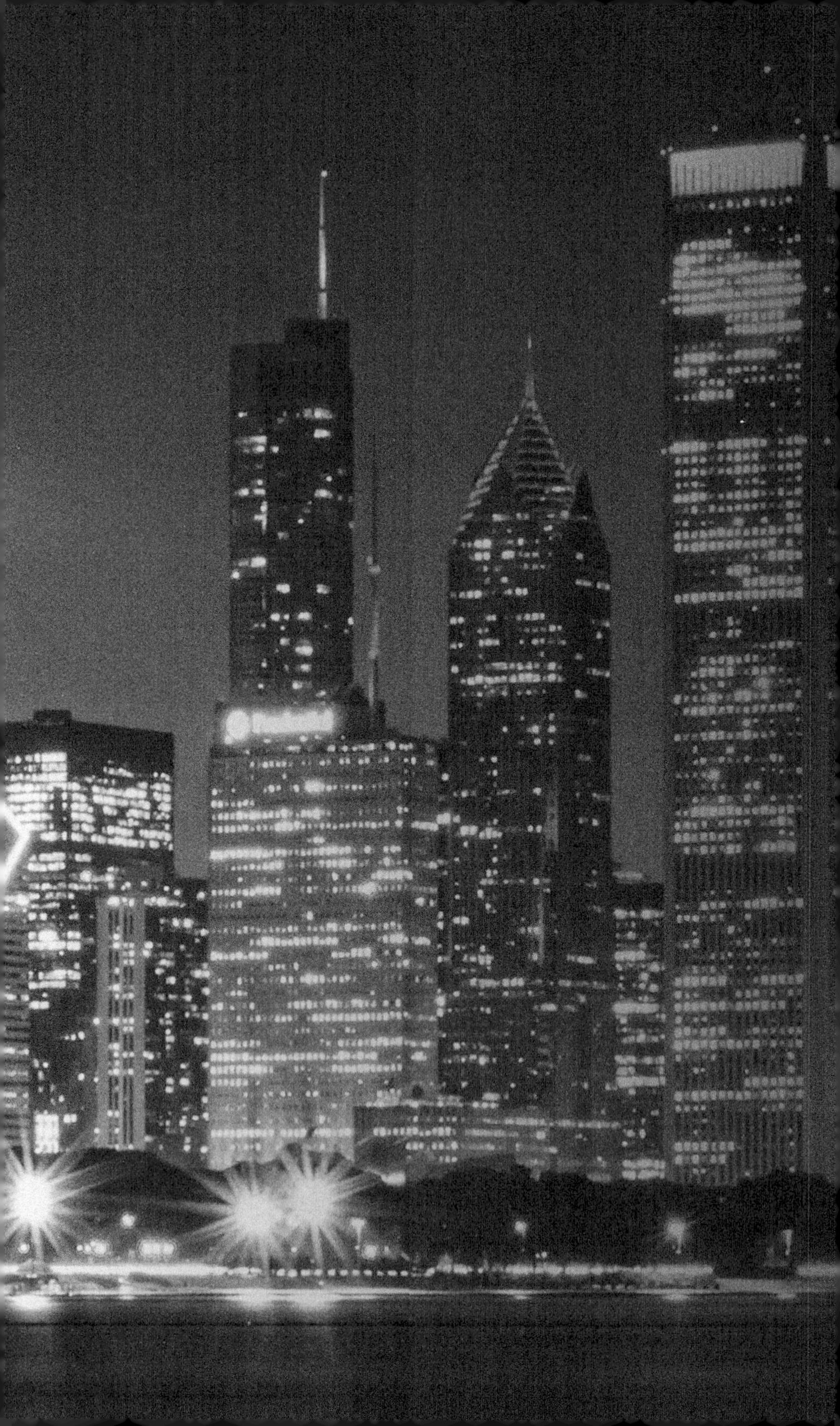

Chapter Two

Alessio

"PARANOIA"—A DAY TO REMEMBER

"Something isn't right. I watched her for several days. I followed her to the funeral, then to her condo. Nothing I saw gave me the impression she's a cold, calculating, murderous bitch," I muttered with a sigh as I rested my forearms on my thighs. My brother, Vittorio, quietly waited, letting me work through my frustrations.

I kept it to myself that watching her operate a welder like a boss made her look like a badass to me.

"So watch her for a bit longer," he offered with a shrug. I'd stopped by his office to see him, and he immediately knew I needed to talk.

"After that, I followed her for *four more days*. V, I was on her every move. Walking around town, grocery shopping—you name it. She gave money to the panhandlers, and she bought them food and water. She volunteers at soup kitchens and at animal shelters. Then also finds time to create high-demand art. The woman is practically a paragon," I grumbled, glancing over to stare out the window at the city of Chicago below.

"Maybe it's all an act. Like an illusion to throw people off."

"Maybe. That's why I made the decision to wait. Maybe I'm missing something." Before I completed my mission, I needed to be sure. Yet my client was on my ass. Another thing I didn't like.

"Um, then—"

Stuck in my head, I continued as if he hadn't said anything. "This job has rubbed me wrong from day one, but I had been exhausted after returning to the States and I wasn't thinking clearly."

My brother lifted his brows, and I knew he was thinking what I was. Despite a nine-day assignment over in Japan, I couldn't afford to be less than razor sharp. I'd been sleep deprived and my brain hadn't caught up with me. In a particularly cold and dead space in my head, I let the client talk me into something I never did.

That's where things got me in trouble. Facet had told me he got a weird vibe off this case, because the client wouldn't say who the target was until she talked to me directly. But because he had told me the client wanted her husband's murderer eliminated, I had no qualms. Hell, I thought it would be an easy job. After all, the person lived right here in Chicago.

It would pay well.

Quick cash. No travel.

It was a no-brainer. What I hadn't realized until she

Blood TIES

called my burner to discuss the details of the job was that the target was her stepdaughter.

That made me initially pause, though I didn't hit the brakes.

I mean, I had two rules.

Number one, I didn't work for my family. Like ever. If they wanted someone dead, they had their ways. Not to say I wouldn't put a bullet between someone's eyes if I needed to—because I had and would again in a heartbeat. Because let someone threaten my family... what's that saying? Fuck around and find out?

Number two, I didn't kill kids. In the Army, I'd had been forced to do just that and I hated it. But that was a situation where I was faced with the impossible choice to take out the kid with enough explosives strapped to him to level a small city, or my entire team was dead. That was the day I learned to shut off my emotions.

There was one more thing—and this was where this job became a problem. If one wanted to get technical, I had a third rule, but it was… flexible. I didn't kill women. Unless they were straight up evil cunts—E.C.'s. And believe me, they existed.

But this chick? After watching her—*seeing* her—she wasn't one. No way.

I liked to think I had incredibly accurate instincts—they'd kept me alive on numerous occasions. Every single fiber of my being knew something wasn't jiving.

The woman that hired me? If what I was thinking was true, I'm pretty sure she fit in that E.C. category.

I didn't like being lied to. In fact, I hated it. I especially didn't like being lied to about a target. It was one reason I was so meticulous with my job. If the target wasn't easily researched or publicly know, I watched them for about a week. I needed to know their habits—their routines. I didn't like being caught with my pants down. Well, unless my cock was out and in a woman's mouth.

But I digress.

The E.C. who hired me had sent what she claimed was email traffic between the target and another person discussing how to kill her biological father. Then pictures of a raven-haired beauty that had called to me in a weird way that I'd ignored—or tried to. In the still photos, she was definitely slipping something out of her bag and into Justin Santino's drink while he had left the table for a phone call.

It made me question my gut feelings, and I hated it.

Facet had verified that the emails originated from her condo.

The problem was, Justin's death had been ruled a massive heart attack. But he'd been cremated before any toxicology reports could be run. Supposedly, it had been his request that he be immediately cremated, but fuck.

"So you think your client is lying?" Vittorio asked. He and Gabriel were the only ones I ever discussed any of my jobs with. And I was selective with that.

"I could be wrong, but yeah."

"What are you going to do?"

"I'm going to check into a few things. Then, I'm gonna get closer to her."

"The target or the bitch that hired you? Either way, are you sure that's a good idea?" He cocked a brow and gave me the look that said he thought I was nuts.

"I have to, V. I won't pull the trigger without knowing the truth." I fell back in the chair and ran my hands over my face in frustration. "I should've never agreed to this. I fucking knew better."

I was worried I was slipping.

"You know, you don't need to do this anymore. You've made enough money to live comfortably for the rest of your life," Vittorio murmured, trying to sound off the cuff.

"It's not about the money," I argued, dropping my hands to my lap. Okay, real talk? Initially, it was absolutely about the money. When I'd gotten out of the Army, I was completely cold, heartless, and devoid of emotions. I didn't give a rat's ass about the details of why someone wanted some dude dead. That wasn't my concern. I had a job to do.

Now? I was losing my edge.

"Then what? Do you truly love killing people?" Again with the questioning my sanity look.

"Do you?" I shot back. My brother easily had as much blood on his hands as I did.

He cocked a brow and tipped his chin up. "Touché."

"It's no different than what The Family has to do. It's business. Not to mention, most of the assignments I accept are about erasing people that do revolting and hateful things without conscience. There are too many people who get away with sick shit."

"Right, but the boys down in Ankeny take care of that, too."

"True, but fuck, they can't do it all. Most of mine are international, higher-profile targets that they don't usually mess with." We dealt in apples and oranges.

I'd joined the Army with a ranger contract the day I turned eighteen. Our grandfather had been pissed, but I didn't give two shits then and I didn't now. He was the biggest reason I wanted the fuck out of Chicago at the time, and one of the reasons I didn't work for my family. Our dad completely understood, and I was thankful for him—I just wish he'd stood up to our grandfather more for us over the years.

After completing twenty-two weeks of OSUT—One Station Unit Training—I went to Airborne School. Talk about an adrenaline rush. Not that it was a cakewalk, but it was slightly easier than RASP—Ranger Assessment and Selection Program.

What RASP really boiled down to was eight weeks where they weeded out the soldiers that didn't have the physical or mental capacities to be a Ranger. In other words, it was fucking brutal. That's where I first met Facet—Damien Blackwood.

Because I refused to fail and have my grandfather gloat, I made it through that eight-weeks of hell and the second I could, I dropped my packet for Special Ops. Facet was right by my side. It had been grueling and fucked with my head, but I made it through selection and was picked up.

What I found out was that we had the opportunity and means to take out so many targets that were a pestilence to humankind and yet our hands were tied. Aggravated didn't come close to describing the feeling that gave me. I was sickened by our impotence in certain situations.

And I'd complained about it within the trusted circle of my team.

After I got out, one of my old battle buddies from the team approached me and made me an offer. That battle buddy was Facet. The dude is a genius with computers. Like insanely smart and talented—eerily so. He helped me set everything up on the dark web, and the Huntsman was born. He and I had been working hand in hand ever since.

Facet screened the clients and got them in touch with me if it was something I was interested in taking on. It was because of me that Gabriel and The Family started working with the RBMC—the Royal Bastards MC down in Ankeny, Iowa.

"Well, good luck, but be careful. I don't need some black widow chick—or whatever the hell they call a kid that commits parricide—killing off my little brother. That would bring out a whole other side of me that my fiancée wouldn't approve of." He smirked.

Little did he know, it wasn't him anyone needed to worry about. Because for some insane reason, when I saw my target in the flesh, all I wanted to do was dirty her snow-white skin.

How fucked was that?

The line at the coffee shop was long but I wasn't in a hurry. When I was halfway to the counter, I tapped on the shoulder of the woman in front of me.

She glanced back at me, and it was like a gut punch. The intense blue of her eyes, framed by thick, dark lashes, was spellbinding. Paired with her long, jet-black hair, she was like Snow White personified.

Though I'd been watching her from a distance for over a week, up close, she was stunning. From the distance I'd watched, I knew she was beautiful with smooth, alabaster skin and full, dark-pink lips that I wanted to lean forward and taste. I gave myself a small shake at that unusual thought.

Fucking hell. Yep, definitely losing my edge.

"Excuse me, I hate to bother you, but are you Nivea Bulgari?" I asked with my most apologetic but hopeful expression.

Her gaze went wary, and I didn't blame her, because the Huntsman was tapping on her door. She just didn't know it. "Umm...."

"You probably think I'm some psycho. I'm sorry. I'm Nick Bowman and I'm a huge fan of your work."

Her shoulders instantly relaxed and a soft pink flush spread over her cheeks. "Really?"

"Yes, really. As a matter of fact, I was thinking of reaching out to you to commission one of your pieces for my parents' restaurant. Imagine how lucky I felt when I realized it was you in line," I poured on the charm, but with a twist of geeky as I pushed up the glasses I wore. I kinda reminded myself of Clark Kent.

Except the glasses were fake. The act was fake. Hell, all of it was fake.

Well, except my attraction to her. Which had no business in this situation. But, fuck, she was classically and insanely beautiful. And there was something about her that was simply... enthralling.

"Oh! Wow! Well, uh, let me see when I have time available to discuss your idea," she offered as she began to dig through her purse.

"I'd really like to discuss it with you as soon as possible. My parents have their anniversary coming up and I'd love to surprise them with it. If you don't think you'd be able to get it done in time, I would need to know as soon as possible so I could plan something else. Please?" I begged her with my charming devil smile.

She quit rummaging through her bag to glance up at me. "I mean, if you're a little flexible, I can meet you for lunch, I suppose," she conceded, biting her lower lip.

"That would be fantastic," I told her with heavy relief in my tone.

"I can't promise you anything. My schedule is a little wild over the next couple of weeks. How about around three p.m. next door on the Tuesday after next? That way, we miss a lot of the crowd. Unless you'd rather come earlier and risk not getting in," she offered, and I almost choked at her words because, yeah, I'd love to get in and come.

Fuck, good thing I was already going to hell. If I wasn't, I sure would be after those thoughts.

"Three on that Tuesday works." That was still two weeks away, and I cursed in my head.

"Okay. Perfect. Then here's my business card. You can email me, call me, or text me. That's my business line." She held it out and when I reached for it, my fingers brushed hers. The jolting current of electricity that seemed to run between us sent my heart racing and her eyes went wide before she shook it off.

I did the same.

By then, we were at the counter. She placed her order and moved to the side, then I did the same. As we waited, she was going through the calendar on her phone. Because I knew what the fuck I was doing, she didn't realize I could see everything on her screen.

Her thumbs flew over the screen as she put our lunch on her calendar. Then she was going through other appointments. She was volunteering at the soup kitchen tomorrow. My brows knotted together. She had an appointment with her gynecologist the next day. Interesting.

Jesus, Alessio, knock it the fuck off. What the hell are you doing?

Wait. She had a *date* on Saturday? I refused to think about why that grated on my nerves. I didn't even know this chick. Yet I'd been following her around for almost a week.

With that, I had to remind myself that this was a job. That was the whole reason I was following her around. She. Was. My. Target. Christ, maybe it was time for me to retire.

But at twenty-seven years old, I wouldn't know what the hell to do with myself.

The barista called out Nivea's name and the ebony-haired beauty gathered her cup. With a small wave, she flipped her scarf around her neck, lifted the cup to her plush lips, and left the coffee shop.

When my order was ready, I nodded to the barista and went outside. As I watched the crowd swallow up the beautiful artist I'd been speaking to, I also lifted my cup to my lips. Steam rose from the opening of the lid. Then I dropped the full cup in the nearest trash and kept walking.

I had a lot to do.

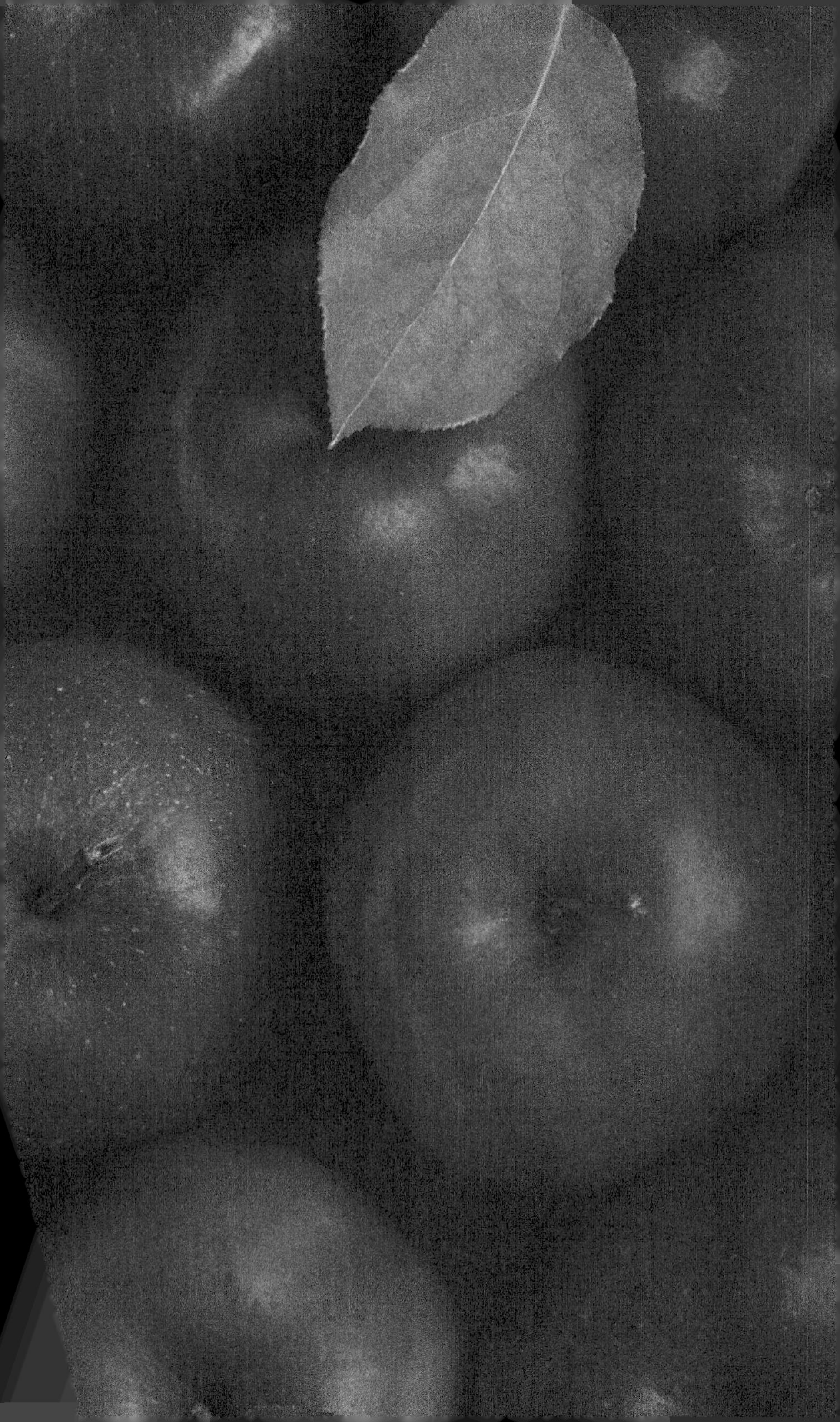

Chapter THREE

Nivea

"BLACK OUT DAYS"—PHANTOGRAM

I was exhausted. I hadn't slept much since the day of Justin's—my biological father's—funeral. For one, how does a guy who seemed so damn fit and healthy die of a damn heart attack? Out of nowhere.

One day you're having lunch with your newfound biological father. Then….

BAM!

Dead.

It just didn't make sense.

The email I'd received from Justin's attorney asking me to come down to his office on Friday was another stressor. Why would he need to talk to me? I had no control or shares in any of Justin's businesses.

A quick glance in the mirror by my door was one last reminder that I looked like shit. With a slump in my shoulders, I dug in my bag for my concealer. After finally locating it at the very bottom, mixed with a bunch of pens and random crap, I dabbed some under my eyes.

"Useless," I muttered and dropped it back in the deep dark hole that was my purse and left my loft.

Me: I'm coming

Nick: Already?

A flicker of something dark and lusty made me ache deep between my legs. With that throbbing awareness, I chewed on my lip, debating whether to reply or let that go unanswered.

Me: Maybe ;)

My heart was pounding as I raced down the sidewalk, my feet hitting the cold ground hard. I was late as it was and, of course, everyone and their brother decided to be out and about. Dodging and weaving, I hurried toward the little cafe to meet with my potential client.

A client I'd been exchanging increasingly unprofessional text messages with since we met two weeks ago. They weren't blatantly sexual but the innuendos—oh, God, the innuendos. That last one was not the worst of them, either.

Looking back, I couldn't say how it started or what had driven either of us. After all, I didn't know him, nor did he know me.

I refused to acknowledge that I was more upset that I looked like roadkill than that I was going to be late. Because Nick was jaw-dropping hot.

By the time I practically skidded to a halt outside the little cafe, I had loose tendrils that had worked free from my messy bun, and I was probably sweaty and nasty. Inwardly, I groaned.

"I'm so sorry I'm late," I apologized as I dropped into the

only free seat at his table. He'd chosen one of the outdoor seats near the propane heaters and shaded by big red umbrellas. I could see why every table inside was packed.

So much for avoiding the busy time.

He pushed the dark frames of his glasses up and I practically fell into his mesmerizing eyes. Crystal blue, with a navy border and striations, they were like a vortex sucking me under. "You're fine," he assured with a kind, but slightly wolfish grin.

Oh God, were those dimples that just flashed with that panty-melting smile?

It took everything I had in me to pull myself together into something that somewhat resembled a professional woman. I had to fight the urge to crawl into his lap and do very bad things—things our messages had flirted with but left unsaid.

Jesus, we're in public! Pull yourself together, girl!

It was one thing to exchange some suggestive text messages, but being in his physical presence was lethal. My face and my insides warmed at the memories. Still, I couldn't let that drive me to do something foolish.

The waitress arrived at my side, causing me to jump when she asked if we were ready to order. I frowned because I hadn't even ordered a drink. But when I looked up, she only had eyes for my table companion.

Which really irked me for some reason—like I had a claim to him.

"Nivea, what did you want to drink?" Nick asked. I

wanted to kiss him for being observant and ignoring the waitress's blatant dismissal of me.

"A water is fine, and I'd like the daily special, please," I replied.

She didn't even acknowledge me, despite the fact that I'd seen her take down my order. Her brilliant smile was for Nick.

"I'll take the same," he said, handing her his menu, then summarily dismissing her as he leaned forward on the table. His attention was one hundred percent focused on me. "I'm glad you could make it."

My cheeks heated at his unwavering focus. Those messages swirled in my brain. Then I pulled out my small sketchbook and a mechanical pencil. "So what were you thinking?"

"That you are utterly stunning," he murmured.

Struck speechless, I couldn't do anything but blink at him as my cheeks went from heated to up in flames. My mouth opened and closed, but no words came out.

He chuckled before bashfully ducking his head. "I'm sorry, that was rude."

"No, I, uh, wow, I'm flattered. Thank you," I stammered. Yeah, in person, he was much more potent.

"Well, it's the truth, but you were referring to what I had in mind for the piece I'd like to commission." He proceeded to explain his vision and I sketched as he spoke. Every so often, he would lean in and point at something, causing our hands to brush together. By the time he was done, I was flustered and horny, but I had a simple drawing that I slid over for him to look at.

"Something like this?" I asked, heart fluttering. He leaned

over to look, and I caught a whiff of his crisp, but mysterious cologne and I dropped my pencil. It rolled off the table and to the ground.

"Crap," I whispered as I quickly bent to pick it up.

I didn't get to sit back up because there was an odd sound and bits of brick rained down on me. Simultaneously, Nick dragged me to the concrete. People were screaming and chairs fell over as chaos ensued.

Nick was intently scanning the area as he kept us hidden behind the table. His glass on the table shattered and water went everywhere. He cursed.

"We have to go," he snapped as he grabbed my hand, then my bag.

I was frozen in place.

"Nivea!" he shouted.

Trembling, I slowly turned to look at him.

"I need you to stay down the best you can and we're going around the side of the building. Okay?"

Numbly, I nodded.

"Go!" he shouted as he grabbed the edge of the table and tipped it. As I scrambled around the corner of the building, I was vaguely aware that he'd used the umbrella as a screen to hide our movements.

Once he was next to me, he didn't dawdle. He clutched my hand, and we ran down the alley. I was barely conscious of where we were going, I simply tried to keep up. I slipped on a patch of ice and he grabbed me to keep me upright. We broke out of the other end on a smaller side street and he pulled me along. A black car skidded to a halt and a man in sunglasses got out.

There was another odd pinging and I shrieked as a window next to us exploded.

"Fuck!" Nick grumbled, then we were darting into a dry cleaners and rushing past the counter. The two people working there shouted, but we kept moving. The rapid pounding of feet behind us gave me a boost of adrenaline and I pushed myself and my burning muscles.

In and out of businesses, we raced. It seemed the pounding footsteps were falling further and further behind, but maybe that was wishful thinking.

Finally, we ducked into a small Italian restaurant. Where the back door was marked as an emergency exit, rather than use it, he quickly darted us into the bathroom and locked the door. He ripped a cell phone out of his pocket and made a call.

Trying to suck air into my lungs, I heard him quietly saying something about help and a car and then gave the name of the restaurant. I couldn't hear much else because of the blood pounding in my head.

He shoved my bag at me that I hugged to my aching chest. He then began pulling things off of a shelf over the toilet and I realized there was a window.

"W-W-What are y-y-y-you doing?" I stuttered through my gasping breaths.

"Trying to get us the hell out of here!" he whisper-yelled as rolls of paper towels and toilet paper went by the wayside.

He unlocked the window and quietly tried to push it open. It wouldn't budge. I wanted to cry.

Then he whipped out a knife that flew open with a soft click. He slid it along the seam of the panes. Once he'd sliced through the paint, he retracted the blade and tucked it back in his jacket. The glasses went with it.

I watched the muscles bulge under the expensive fabric of his coat and the window creaked before it finally opened. The cold winter wind rushed in. He looked both ways outside, then fiddled with the screen until it came loose, and he tilted it as he brought it inside and set it by the toilet.

"I'll go out first and I'll help you down. Okay?" Nick softly instructed.

I simply stood there, shaking.

"Nivea. You have to listen to me. We can't stay here."

I rapidly nodded.

He quickly hoisted himself up to the opening, and then carefully crawled out and dropped to the ground below. As I peeked out, I saw it wasn't too far, but farther than I'd be able to reach.

"I've got you," he reiterated.

First, I passed my bag out to him. Then I used the toilet as a step up. As I stared down at him, I realized I didn't know this guy.

At all.

"Nivea," he urged, staring up at me. He glanced both ways down the alleyway.

The bathroom knob rattled and my breath seized. That was followed by a pounding on the wood that shook the entire frame. Fear held me in its relentless grip.

"Niv!"

There was arguing on the other side about not trashing their restaurant. It sounded like an employee and someone else. Then there was an odd popping sound before something heavy hit the floor and someone slammed against the door.

I decided on the lesser of two evils for the time being and crawled out the window. Firm hands grabbed my hips and lowered me to the ground. Without a second's pause to catch a breath, we were on the move again.

At the end of the narrow alley, a dark car stopped. The passenger window rolled down and the guy in the passenger seat stared at us. I dug in my heels, prepared to run the other way, but Nick's hand held firm and he stopped me. "It's okay."

Two heartbeats and we were on the move again. Once we reached the car, he opened the door and I dove into the warm interior. He was right behind me. As we peeled away from the curb, I saw someone stick their head out of what looked like that bathroom window.

It all happened so fast, but I could've sworn we made eye contact, though that had to be impossible because the windows were tinted dark as night.

"What the hell is going on? Were they shooting at you or me?" I demanded, pushing my fear back down my throat. It was impossible to slow my breathing down and my heart was pounding.

"I have no idea who that was, but I think we need to talk."

"No shit!" I shouted, my heart trying to bust through my ribs.

"Someone is trying to kill you."

My mouth fell open and I stared at the man I believed

I was meeting to discuss commissioning a sculpture. "Who are you?"

He ran a hand through his dark hair, leaving it sexily tousled. There was an obvious internal struggle going on before he steadily met my gaze.

"Who I am doesn't really matter. But I know that someone has a hit out on you."

"We were supposed to be meeting about my art and now you're telling me I'm the target for some hitman?" I was practically shouting, but neither he nor the two men in the front seat seemed fazed by my tone. "Where are you taking me?"

"Somewhere safe," he vaguely replied.

"Did my father hire you?"

Nick's attention snapped to me and his dark brows were pulled down as he silently studied me. Through it all, he remained mute, but his expression told me his answer was no.

"I need to call my dad," I muttered and wildly dug through my purse, cursing that I couldn't have brought something small today. Before I could find the stupid electronic device, Nick was placing a hand on my purse, pressing down to still my search. Then he pulled my bag from my hands.

"You can't call anyone. In fact, I need you to turn your phone off. Now."

"Are you insane?" I blurted out, reaching for my purse. It was imperative that I call my father.

"I wish I were. Now it's either that, or I throw your bag out the window."

"Oh my God. This can't be happening." My parents were incredibly wealthy. It didn't make sense that someone would try to kill me when they could hold me for ransom instead. Unless this wasn't about money. From what I'd gathered over the years, my dad had a lot of enemies.

"My dad is gonna lose his shit," I muttered. He'd been against me moving to Chicago for school and he'd really hated it when I wanted to stay. He'd wanted to hire a security team for me, but Mom and I convinced him that wouldn't be necessary.

"What?" Nick seemed confused.

"Nothing. Fine. Shut it off."

Somehow, he opened the top of my purse, reached in, and immediately found my phone and shut it off. I had no idea how he did that with everything I had in there.

He dropped it back in, then he was on his phone, furiously typing away.

"How is it okay for you to be on yours?" I huffed as I crossed my arms over my chest. "And how do I know you're not kidnapping me?"

A humorless laugh was his initial reply. Then he looked up from his phone and his unearthly blue eyes locked on me. "Because my phone is disposable and because I said I'm not."

A burner? I knew what kind of people had burner phones. Unease settled in my guts. I glanced out the window trying to see if I could tell where we were. *Maybe I can jump out and run.*

"Don't," he grunted without looking at me.

My gaze narrowed on him for his ability to read my mind, but I still debated. Except before I could possibly make

Blood TIES

my escape, we were turning into an underground parking garage. The driver brought us right to the elevator.

"This is us," Nick explained and climbed out of his side. He held a hand in to help me out.

"I need to call my dad," I insisted before I would take it. For some crazy reason I trusted him, but I still had my priorities.

"Fine, but I'll tell you what you can and can't say."

I glared at him but took his hand and followed him out. We got on the elevator and he used his thumbprint to choose a floor. Neither of the two guys came with us.

In the privacy of the enclosed space, he backed me against the wall as he stared intently into my eyes. "It's very important that you do as I say. I'm doing my best to keep you safe right now."

He was so close, I could see every detail of his beautiful eyes, count every thick, dark lash. My nose could trail over the dark scruff that dusted his jawline if I leaned my head in. Pressure squeezed my chest and between my legs tingled. This was so not the time.

"Nick?" I whispered in confusion at how I was feeling after we'd just been chased across downtown.

"Jesus Christ. Stop that shit," he muttered as he frowned and took a quick step away from me. "Pull yourself together."

Like I was the only one who was affected?

"You're a dick." This wasn't the same guy I'd been exchanging sexually charged text messages with over the past week.

"I've heard that before."

"Your name isn't Nick, is it?"

"Nope." The elevator stopped and he guided me off and then to one of two doors on the floor.

"Is it Dick?" I curled my lip.

He shot me a deadpan stare, though the corner of his mouth twitched. Then he opened the door, and we entered a bright, spacious condo.

"You live here?" I asked as I scanned the room. My artist's eye made note of the clean, modern lines and the incredible natural light. The furnishings had a decidedly masculine feel to them, but there were little hints of a woman's touch and I wondered who it had been.

He shrugged as he entered the kitchen and rummaged through a drawer.

"Gee, your answers are positively illuminating," I muttered as I rolled my eyes in irritation. Maybe I was being mouthy, but so far, he hadn't done anything to hurt me. And he was letting me call my father, which after what I'd just learned, was a necessity.

Finally, he clicked a battery into a cheap phone and set it on the counter. He gestured toward it.

Cautiously, I shuffled closer and reached for it. Keeping an eye on him, I dialed my dad's number, praying he'd answer.

"Put it on speaker. Tell him you're safe and you'll call him when you can."

"Sure." I did as I was told.

"Yes?" My father's voice was brusk and all business, likely because he didn't know the number.

"Dad?"

"Nivea. Whose phone is this?" All traces of my usual jokester dad were gone. This was the all-business dad.

"A friend's," I replied. "I lost my phone, so I'm using theirs."

"Who's the friend?" I could hear my dad furiously typing. Considering my dad knew I had exactly seven friends here, and he knew everything about them, I had a feeling I knew what he was doing. I'd had the same friends since college where we'd all met and, though we were a motley bunch, we were close.

I glanced at Not-Nick and gave him a questioning stare.

He wrote on a piece of paper.

A guy you started seeing

I choked.

"Niv?" Concern and irritation bled through the line. My dad was not happy.

I sighed. "It's a guy I've been seeing," I said with resignation.

Silence.

"A guy?"

Shit.

Shit. Shit. Shit.

"Yeah, Dad. A guy." I closed my eyes, waiting for the explosion.

"You have got to be fucking kidding me, Niv. We have talked about this time and time again." Someone who didn't know my dad would think that was a calmly stated reply. Those of us who knew him knew there were a million nukes going off in his brain. We had a procedure if I was even *thinking* about seeing a guy.

"Dad, it's new," I whispered as I leaned close to the phone. Not like that kept my new "guy" from hearing it, but Jesus, I was embarrassed as hell. I'd blocked the trauma of being shot at and chased halfway across Chicago, but this was putting a strain on that box I'd carefully packed it into.

I burst into tears.

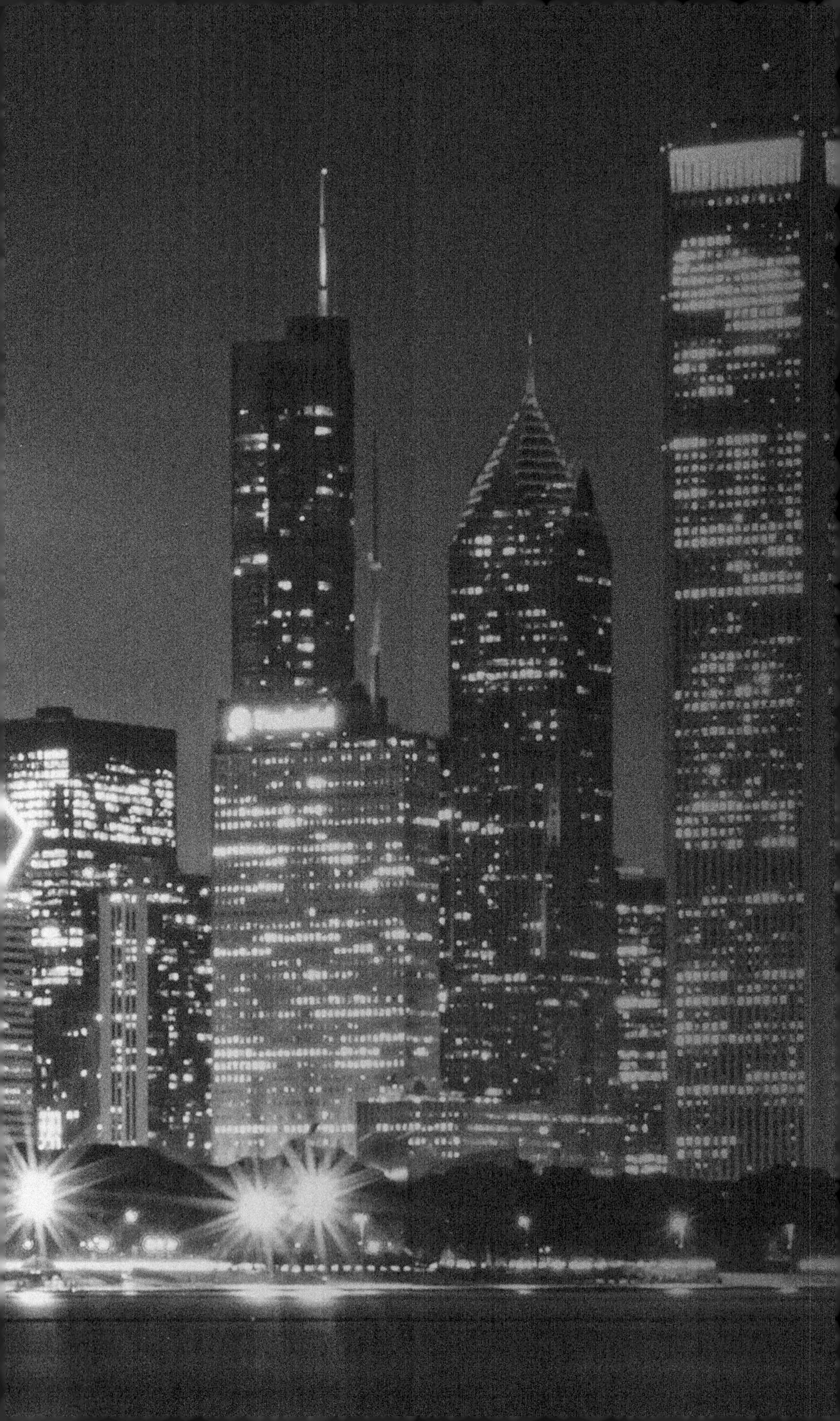

Chapter Four

Alessio

"EVERYTHING CHANGES"—STAIND

Fuck.

"Niv? What the hell is going on?" Nivea's father shouted through the phone.

She had dropped onto one of my barstools and her face was buried in her hands. I wasn't sure if I should try to comfort her or what the fuck to do. I didn't deal well with emotions like that. I was an organizer—a planner. I was a fixer, but shit, I didn't know her like that.

And I was afraid to get too close to her, because in the elevator, I'd nearly fucked up. I couldn't start blurring the lines any worse than they already were. The text messages that had started as a ploy to work my way into her head had somehow become more.

They'd become real.

And I found myself liking her more than I should.

Finally, I picked up the phone and took it off speaker. "Sir?"

Initially, there was no reply. I looked at the screen and

it still showed I was on an active call. Before I could say anything else, Nivea's father spoke. His tone was calm and cold.

"You took the phone off speaker?"

"Yes."

"Who the fuck are you and why did my daughter just call me from a burner phone?"

I was a little taken aback. Once I shook off that uncharacteristic feeling, I wondered how the hell this guy knew that. The whole purpose of a burner was anonymity.

"My name is Alessio." I gave him that much. And quite frankly, I wasn't sure why I gave him my real first name other than I figured there were a million guys with the name Alessio in the world.

"And how do you know my daughter?"

"Well, I met her when we discussed commissioning a sculpture for my parents' restaurant," I replied. After all, that wasn't completely untrue.

The unmistakable sound of fingers rapidly typing on a keyboard could be heard as I waited for his response. "And why is my daughter crying?"

"That's kind of a long story," I stalled. Why did I feel like the tables were being turned on me?

"I have time," he clipped.

If I told him what had really happened, he'd want us to call the police. That was the general population's knee-jerk reaction. That was the last thing this situation needed because I didn't have any idea who the key players were or who was involved.

"Sir, your daughter is safe. She's in a highly secure

building in Chicago. There was an incident that was a little nerve-racking, but we're at my condo and I promise you she will not be harmed in any way while I'm here."

"That. Doesn't. Comfort. Me."

"I underst—"

"No, you don't. Because that is *my* daughter, not yours. My daughter called me on a throwaway phone, then started crying. You get on the phone and I still don't know who you are. I'm not the one to fuck with here. So *Alessio*, I want a last name and an address of where my daughter is. Right the fuck now. Am I clear?"

That wasn't the response of a man ready to call the cops.

Fucking hell, if I gave him my last name, there was no way a search wouldn't show who my family was—in fact, it would probably pop up with flashing lights and sirens. Despite the fact that I wasn't officially tied to *La Cosa Nostra* through my brothers, the De Luca name wasn't one that slipped easily under the radar. Especially not for a guy who knew this was a burner.

"Tick-tock, Alessio. Because I'm already on my way to the airport and if I have to track you down, you're going to wish you hadn't been born. And in case you have any doubts, I *will* track you down."

I'd had enough of this shit. I turned my back to Nivea and quietly snapped out my reply.

"I don't think *you* understand… this is *my* house, *my* town, and *I'm* calling the shots. Nivea is safe. She sure as fuck wasn't earlier, but I can promise you she is now. If you contact the police, I can't guarantee that will remain the case as I don't know where they stand," I bit out, my blood boiling.

"You are a dead man if I don't have a name and a location," he ground out through obviously gritted teeth. Christ, I could hear the grind of his molars over the phone.

Let him come for me. I'd faced a helluva lot worse than some rich guy in California could dish out.

"My name is Alessio De Luca." I rattled off the address as I heard a gasp and glanced over my shoulder at Nivea. She sat there with her mouth hanging open and tears still staining her now blotchy, but still beautiful, red face.

Fuck.

"I—" he started, then paused. The steam coming off him practically singed me through the damn phone.

Other than I was pissed, and I *dared* this motherfucker to come up into my town and threaten me, I had no earthly idea why I gave him my real name. Shit, this was bad. I didn't lose my cool like that.

But hell if this raven-haired beauty wasn't fucking up my normally meticulous and calculated world.

Though I knew the security of our building was damn near impenetrable, this guy already talked a mad game. I needed to know who the hell he was exactly, and what he was capable of.

"Your name, so I can tell my doorman?" I asked as if I was asking about the weather.

"Matthew Bulgari, and I'll be there tonight. So help me God, if there is a hair on my daughter's head that is out of place, I will end you." He ended the call instead.

"Well, your father is on his way," I brightly announced with a tight, fake smile. Then I quickly shot off a text to Facet. He would know it was me without a doubt. Like I said, he was crazy good at shit.

Me: Who the fuck is Matthew Bulgari, father to Nivea Bulgari?

I was fully confident in my ability to kill without remorse, but this was a goddamn nightmare.

"You're Alessio De Luca?" she whispered, eyes bugging.

I wanted to wince. Instead, I asked, "How do you know who I am?"

Anyone with access to the internet and had any interest in the mafia would know who I was. The question was more to distract her and stall.

"Why did you lie to me?" Wariness crept into her voice and her face went expressionless.

Trying to decide how much to tell her, I strummed my fingers on the countertop. My phone vibrated in my hand and I glanced down.

Facet: Why are you asking?

Me: Because my target is his fucking daughter

Facet: Abort. Jesus fucking Christ. Abort!

Me: Great. Well, she's in my *condo*

Facet: Oh my fuck

My phone rang.
"Yes?"
"Dude."

That was all I heard before Facet's voice cut in and out, then my call cut off. When I tried to call him back, it went straight to voicemail. Several times. Slowly, I set down the phone. Then I focused all of my attention on the beautifully broken woman in my condo.

"Nivea," I calmly drawled, then blinked twice. "Who is your father?"

Eyelashes spiky with her tears, she stared back at me. Her eye twitched and she sniffled.

Chest tight, I stalked to the small table by my door and grabbed a box of tissues. Then I returned to the kitchen and set it in front of her.

"Thanks," she mumbled before plucking a few from the box and blowing her nose in a very unladylike manner. Gross, but I liked it—the fact that she didn't give two shits about being prissy.

"You didn't answer me," I prompted.

"Matthew Bulgari," she warily offered.

"Yes. I know that." I counted to ten and breathed deeply.

"How about you tell me what the hell happened today, Mr. Mafia, and I tell you about my dad?"

"I'm not in the mafia," I grunted.

"Semantics. You're the grandson of a former Chicago Family don, the son of another, and the brother to the current don and his underboss." She gave me a look that clearly said she believed I was splitting hairs.

"Well, looks like you know your mafia lines," I muttered. "Why's that?"

"Does it matter? I'm not wrong, though you've been very

good at keeping any current pictures of yourself off the internet. Now what happened today? Because if I don't have a really good answer for my dad when he gets here, well, let's just say he's very protective of me." She crossed her arms belligerently, though her inhale was shaky—likely from her crying bout.

"How well do you know your stepmother?"

"Besides she's a bitch and I have no idea what Justin saw in her?"

I pressed my lips flat, then tipped my head back to stare heavenward. Then I brought my gaze back to her and bluntly asked, "Did you kill your father—Justin?"

Her jaw came unhinged as she blinked at me, clearly in shock. Then her face went bright red, and I was pretty sure she was looking for something to throw at me. "You really are a fucking dick."

"No, I'm simply trying to get to the bottom of a bucket of bullshit. Your stepmother has email traffic where you were trying to find out about Justin's will. She also has photographic evidence of you putting something in his drink when he left the table. It was timestamped the day before he died," I told her, my jaw ticking in frustration.

To say she was stunned was a gross understatement. Her mouth was flapping like a fish and her hand splayed over her chest.

"She *what?*" she finally choked out.

I sighed. Then I walked out of the room and into my office. I returned with the large envelope that I slapped on the breakfast bar in front of her. She stared askance at it like it was a venomous snake.

"Open it."

With trembling fingers, she lifted the flap and dumped the contents out. One by one, her brows pinched tighter with each page she scanned. "Is this a joke? That's not my email account. And these pictures… totally out of context."

My gaze narrowed as I read every nuance of her body language and features. Every bit of it said she was telling the truth. "That IP address traces to your loft and your laptop. That's definitely you in those images."

"My laptop?" Sheer terror distorted her features. "My loft?"

At first, she looked like she was going to hyperventilate, then she dropped the pages like they burned her. She held a finger up as if she was asking for a minute as she stood and began to pace. The entire time, she was mumbling and holding her hands to her head.

"Nivea?"

She stopped in her tracks and stared at me in pained disbelief. Her shoulders curled in. "Who would do that to me? Why would they make it look like that? And why wouldn't they just go to the police if they thought I killed him? And why do you have all of this?"

If I told her I'd been hired to kill her, that would be the end of this conversation, and possibly the end of my contact with her. At that thought, my stomach churned and my chest seized. "You obviously know my family. Let's just say I have information from a reliable source that your stepmother hired someone to kill you because you killed Justin to get his money."

"We met for lunch. He told me he had been suffering from a terrible headache. I told him I had an herbal blend that works wonders. He got a phone call that he excused himself for, and I mixed it up for him. He was aware, though. I have more in my bag—you can look." She gestured toward her gigantic purse that sat on the end of the kitchen counter.

When I did just that, she murmured, "Zippered inside pocket."

Exactly where she'd said, there were several small, folded parchment paper packets. Opening one, I found what looked like finely crushed herbs. A brief, curious sniff didn't tell me exactly what they were. "You care if I have these looked at?"

"Knock yourself out," she emotionlessly replied.

As I messaged my brother Gabriel, I kept an eye on her. She slowly glided over to the wall of glass in the living room.

"Can I ask you a question?" Her question was so softly spoken, at first, I wasn't sure she was talking to me.

"What question?" I warily countered.

"The messages… and when you said you thought I was stunning, was that just part of your act?" she asked as she hugged herself and stared out of the window.

Maybe it was how lost and wounded she appeared. Maybe I was truly losing my edge. Or maybe I was simply a fucking idiot.

Regardless of the reason, my reply wasn't in words. I stalked across the room until she turned to face me as I closed in. When it was obvious I wasn't stopping, she backed up until her spine was to the glass.

Leaning in and bringing my face close until my nose nearly touched hers, I braced my hands on the cool glass by her head. I stared into her startled gaze. "You are the most beautiful woman I've ever seen. I've been attracted to you since the moment I had you in my sights. If things had been different, I would've brought you here and fucked you until your voice was hoarse from screaming my name. Does that answer your question?"

The text messages we'd shared for two weeks had been the first of my bad decisions, yet I wouldn't take it back for anything in the world. Initially, they were simply supposed to be carefully planted seeds of trust and familiarity. They had quickly morphed into something I didn't recognize—like I truly was Nick Bowman.

A different man entirely.

All day, every day, I checked my phone like some kid—hoping and praying she'd replied. Hoping I hadn't gone too far with my suggestive comments. Obviously not, because somehow they had led us to this tense, heated place.

Her breath came in short pants that blew over my lips. I wasn't prepared for her moving into my space, but I sure as hell didn't waste time debating when she did. The second her lips brushed mine, I tilted my head and swept my tongue into her mouth.

She curled her fingers into my shirt, clutching the fabric tightly.

Claiming and devouring, our tongues swirled and stroked

as I learned every contour in her mouth and tasted her desire. I kept my hands on the window until hers began to rapidly unbutton my shirt. The second her soft hands slipped inside and splayed on my chest, I lost my stoic battle. I slid one into the gap left by the curve of her back and down to grip her ass. When I jerked her close so she could feel what she did to me, she gasped against my lips.

"Does that answer your question?" I asked against her still open mouth.

Three heartbeats.

A few more.

"I need you," she whispered.

My heart thundered and I dropped my forehead to hers. It took Herculean effort to get my dick to chill out. "This is a colossally bad idea—it's the adrenaline. I'm not going to do something you'll regret."

"Why don't you let me worry about what I will or won't regret," she murmured as she nuzzled the tip of her nose along mine. Her soft, full lips grazed the corner of my mouth and then my cheek.

My self-restraint was dwindling and my lust was already on a tight leash, but at her words, I let it run wild. Pure need roared through my veins as I roughly removed her clothes. As each inch of her ivory skin was revealed, I kissed, nipped, and licked every luscious curve along the way. A little voice in my head tried to warn me, but I ignored it.

Bad idea. Such a bad, bad idea.

On my hands, I could practically see the metaphoric blood that was there. The contrast of my darkness against the purity of her pale skin was almost obscene. I had no business touching her, but yet I did it anyway.

By the time I tugged her pants down her legs, I was on my knees. She pushed my shirt over my shoulders and I shrugged it off, letting it fall forgotten to the floor.

As my palms smoothed up the outside of her thighs, I trailed my tongue up the insides until I reached her apex. Frustrated that her pants still held her legs together, I removed her shoes and peeled off her leggings. Once I lifted one leg and placed it over my shoulder, it beautifully displayed her and allowed me to dip into her heated core.

She reached out to grab my shoulders for balance.

After one single swipe through her pussy, I paused long enough to moan, "Jesus, that's good." Then I was swiping my greedy tongue through her soaked cleft and plunging into her tight sheath, the way I wanted to do with my aching cock.

This was reckless and crazy, but hell if I could stop. One taste and I was a junkie for her exquisite and unique essence.

She had her hands tangled in my hair as she scraped her short nails along my scalp. I practically purred at the feeling.

"God, Alessio, that feels… amazing," she breathlessly admitted as she shamelessly ground her clit against the pressure of my ever-moving tongue. She chanted "so good" over and over until a soft cry fell from her lips and she flooded my face with her release. It ran down my chin as I sucked every drop I could from her soaking, throbbing cunt.

"Fuck, that was beautiful," I ground out before I bit her pussy lip playfully.

She tugged at my hair and I stood up, wiping my mouth

on my upper arm as I did. Our gazes held as I unbuckled my pants and deftly unfastened them. They dropped to the ground, and I kicked them away before I shoved my boxer briefs down to free my cock. Slowly, I stroked my length, twisting my wrist each time I reached the head.

"Are you sure?" I asked, as if some minuscule, sane part of me knew this was insanity.

Her pink tongue swept over her full bottom lip. "Yes. Please."

"What do you want?" I asked her.

"I know I must be out of my goddamn mind, but I want you inside me. I *need* you inside me."

At that, my dick jumped and pulsed in my grip. Not waiting a second for her to change her mind, I released it long enough to grab her ass and lifted her up. She hooked her legs around my hips, and I used the floor to ceiling windows and one hand to balance her while I lined myself up with her slick flesh. She was still so wet that I slid right in. A few strokes and I was buried balls deep. She was so hot and tight around me, I lost myself a little.

Breathing became a task.

Conscious thought, what was that? A distant memory of something, obviously.

With her hips in my hands and her legs around my waist, I drove hard up into her. She moved up the glass and her nails scored the flesh of my shoulder. Teeth bared, I hissed in a sharp breath. Several more times brought me closer to the promise of ecstasy.

"Yes! Oh God, yes!" Her cry filled my condo as I filled

her over and over until we were nothing more than an animalistic combination of sweaty limbs and desperate need. Each thrust slammed my pelvis to her swollen clit, and I ground against her every time.

Her body stiffened as if it knew to brace itself for what was barreling down on us.

Then, her hot cunt tightened around me, squeezing harder until it contracted and throbbed around me.

I gritted my teeth as I fought to keep myself in check. Once I was sure I had control, I pulled out and she whimpered. "Turn around. Hands on the glass," I demanded, and she immediately complied. "Good girl," I whispered.

This end of the condo offered the same stunning view of Millennium Park that Vittorio and Gabriel's condos shared. It was unlikely anyone could see us, but the thrill that someone might had my cock aching to be back inside her.

The sight of her curvy hips made my fingers flex. Reaching out and grabbing her in a bruising grip, I pulled them toward me until her ass jutted out and her glistening pink pussy called to me. The Chicago view framing her ivory body was breathtaking. "Fuck, that's hot."

She glanced over her shoulder, and I was a goner. Nothing that had happened earlier in the day mattered as I lined up and drove deep inside her. It was pure heaven.

"Alessio!" she gasped. The sound of my name on her lips was a potent and deadly thing because I became another person. Driven by sheer lust, I pulled out and fucked her hard. The view outside disappeared as the only one that mattered was her wet pussy squeezing my cock like no one before her ever had.

The slap of damp skin each time I slammed into her only spurred me on. The way her porcelain white ass jiggled with each thrust made me want to mark it up. I gave her a swift smack on one perfect globe and she cried out as she clamped down on me so tight I almost passed out.

"God, do that again," she urged.

Christ, I groaned, but I did as she requested. When she demanded again, I repeated the motion until her skin was rosy red and she was coming like the goddess she was.

When my knees nearly buckled, I braced one hand over hers and our fingers instantly threaded. With my face buried in her neck, I tightened my other arm around her, and cupped one perfect tit.

My balls drew up and I combusted. Cock buried deep and powerfully pulsing, I filled her with my cum.

"That was…." She didn't finish her sentence, but I got it.

Panting hard, I had no words for what had just transpired either. It was crazy hot, and though I realized I fucked up and didn't use a condom, with my current haze of contentment, I couldn't find it in me to care.

As if she read my mind, she gasped, "I have an IUD, but please tell me I don't have to worry about getting something for that stupid move."

"Considering I haven't gone bare in my life, I'd say you should be pretty safe," I replied, my words interspersed with heavy breaths. I kissed the soft slope of her shoulder before I licked up the side of her neck, savoring the salty taste of her skin. When I reached that tender spot behind her ear, she shivered and let out a sexy little gasp.

"Then why now?" she gently pushed me back and turned so I could meet her gaze. I slipped free and I wanted to cry at the loss of her tight heat.

"I have no earthly idea other than you affect my judgement in the craziest ways," I honestly admitted. My head had never been so fucked up in all my life and with my grandfather, that was saying something.

Our grandfather was a sadistic, hateful bastard who had shared a house with my family all my life. Even everything he put us through hadn't broken through my tough outer shell. I'd never let him in to affect my head to the point where I made bad or insane decisions.

"Same," she whispered, the look in her baby blues as confused as I felt.

"You wanna get cleaned up?" I asked her, and she nodded.

I scooped her up and she squeaked, and her arms wrapped around my neck. "I'm too heavy!"

"Do I look like I'm struggling to you? You're fucking perfect," I told her with a smirk. And she was.

We took our time getting cleaned up and we might've gotten dirty and had to wash off again. A small part of me knew this was likely just an unhealthy way to deal with the traumatic events of the day, but it didn't stop me.

As she dried off, I went back to the dining room and grabbed her clothes.

"I have your stuff, or I can get you something to put on," I offered when I returned to the bedroom.

"Um, if you have something, that would be great," she murmured, not making eye contact. That wasn't acceptable.

I placed her things on the bed and pulled her against me. Then I gently lifted her chin, but she closed her eyes. "Look at me," I softly instructed.

She opened her crystalline-blue eyes and slowly lifted her gaze to mine.

"We didn't do anything to be ashamed of. We're both adults and we were both consenting, right?"

Her white teeth sunk into her lip, but she nodded.

"Then don't look like you regret it. Unless you do?"

"No! Of course not! But look at you… and look at me," she mumbled as her brows pulled together.

A frown pulled at my brow because I didn't know what she was talking about. My gaze swept her from head to toe.

"What I see when I look at you is a fucking goddess. Are you hiding a third arm somewhere? Maybe a set of eyes in the back of your head? Because you are by far the most beautiful woman I've ever seen. There was a reason my text messages got a little out of hand this week, you know." She still didn't look like she believed me. "Or is it me? Am I that repulsive?" I teased.

She gave an unladylike snort of laughter. "You? Repulsive? Are you delusional? I'm just sure you're usually with tall, lithe, model-types. Not girls like me."

"Girls like you?" I was truly confused. She was every man's wet dream—iconic bombshell. Curves in all the right places, perfect tits, and an ass that was made for spanking and holding onto while I fucked the hell out of her.

"I'm not exactly skinny," she muttered and gave me a side eye.

"And thank fuck for that," I blurted out, the lightbulb finally going off for me. "Christ, a guy wants a woman like you. I wasn't kidding when I said you're a goddess. You are absolutely gorgeous, and I don't ever want to hear you say otherwise."

Like I would be in her life for much longer.

Because if she found out I'd been hired to kill her, she'd hate me forever.

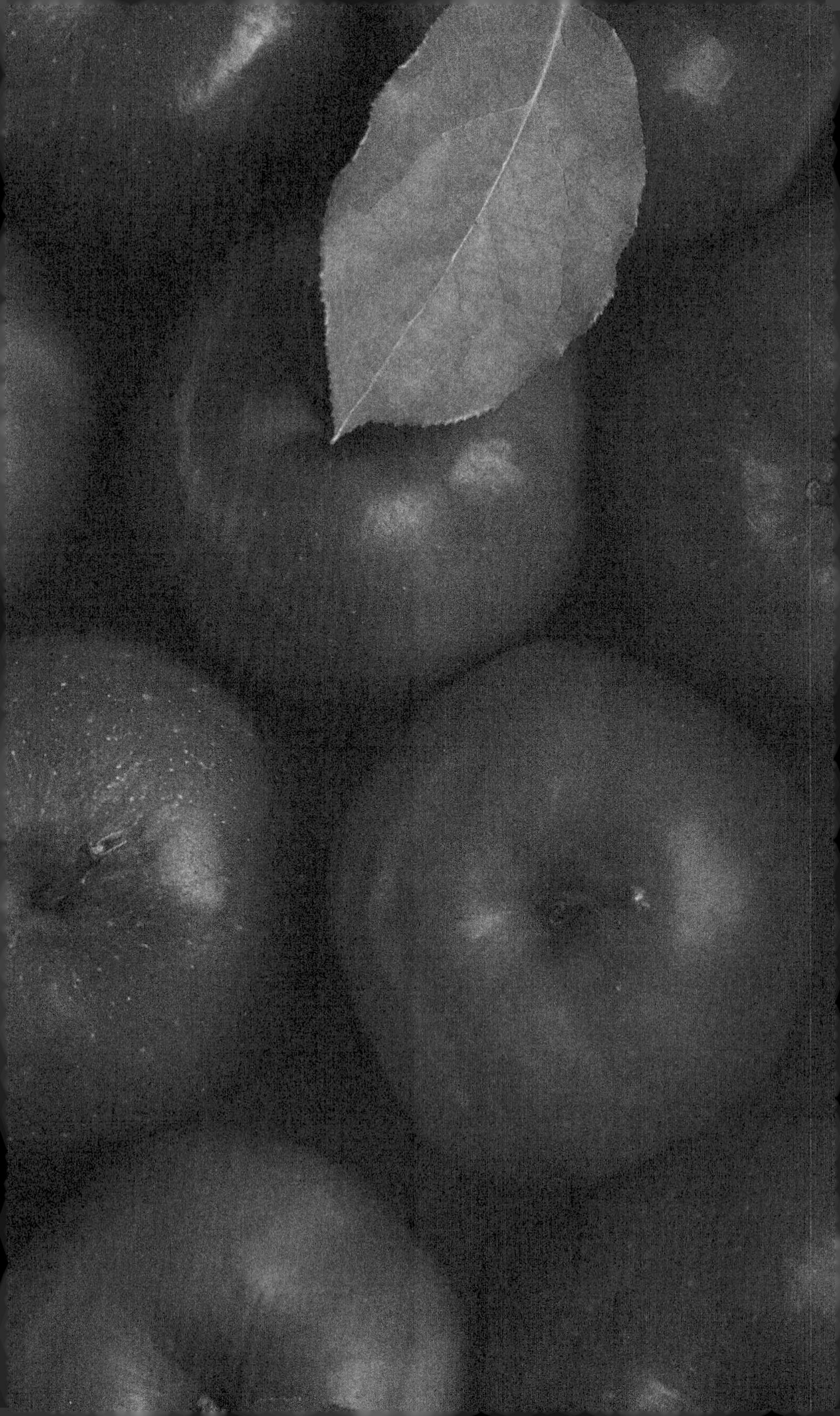

Chapter FIVE

Nivea

"OLDER"—SASHA ALEX SLOAN

"Come out when you're ready," Alessio told me. He left me to get dressed in a dark T-shirt that was soft and smelled like him. The sweats he laid out on the bed were much too long and I had to roll them up. Without clean underwear, I put on my bra and skipped the panties.

I could hear him quietly talking on the phone out in the condo somewhere. It was a soft murmur that I couldn't make out, but it was comforting knowing he was there. I slowly wandered toward the sound of his voice.

No way was he for real. I hadn't had a lot of serious relationships because once guys saw that I was a "thick chick," they tended to ghost me. Most guys that looked like him wanted that lean chick that looked great in a bikini—I was more of a pinup girl on a good day.

I love myself, but I didn't usually get the response that I was getting from Alessio. Maybe over my boobs, but hell, I was curvy. I mean, I like tacos, so I had a bit of a belly. I wasn't friendly with the gym. Not that I hadn't gotten memberships before. But I rarely remembered to eat during the day because I was so absorbed in my work—I sure as hell didn't remember to go to the gym.

He had ended his call and watched me approach. His chin lifted slightly as if… as if he was bracing himself for me to hurt him.

"My father is coming here. I can't let him know about… this," I murmured, self-conscious of what we'd done. I'd never been the kind of girl who was confident in her skin and with the opposite sex.

His beautiful blue eyes shuttered, and I knew I'd done exactly as he had expected.

"Of course." He turned away and faced the darkening skyline. The lights of the surrounding buildings blinked on bit by bit.

A quick glance at the massive clock over the white marble fireplace told me my father would be here soon. My chest ached, but I didn't really know why.

"He would think you took advantage of me," I tried to explain.

He spun on his heel, his features tight. "I get it," he bit out.

"I don't think you do," I tried.

He gave a humorless laugh. "Oh, I think I do. The precious rich princess can't admit to daddy-dearest that she fucked the mafia-born scum. Right?"

The words were cold and hateful, and they hit their mark.

I clenched my jaw and painfully swallowed the lump of glass shards. "That's not true," I argued, my voice breaking.

"Nivea, it doesn't matter."

"Jesus, Alessio, I don't expect you to fall on your knees, professing your love for me. I know damn well that we don't know each other. But don't minimize whatever *that*,"—I waved my hand toward the floor to ceiling windows—"was, by saying hateful things to cover up the fact that you felt it too."

The muscle in his jaw jumped as he clenched his teeth. No words left his lips, refuting what I'd said. The way he cast his gaze away and couldn't meet my eyes told me I was right.

"I'm not the one who wanted to pretend it didn't happen," he finally bit out.

"Alessio…." I wasn't trying to pretend it didn't happen. When I took a step closer, he held up a hand for me to stop. "You're right. That was a… mistake. It shouldn't have happened. Because who I am, what I am, isn't safe for you. You're a good person and regardless of my place with my family, you don't need this in your life."

Though his writing everything off as a mistake hit deep, I refused to allow him to dismiss the almost tangible connection we'd shared. I opened my mouth to continue trying to convince him, but his phone rang and he answered it.

"Yes? Okay, yes. Usual procedure. Send him up," was his part of the conversation. He ended the call and tossed his phone to the coffee table. "Your father is here."

Alessio refused to meet my gaze as we waited. Instead, he busied himself at the bar, setting out crystal glasses that he filled from a cut-crystal decanter. At the knock on the door, he set the bottle down and prowled toward the door.

That was the only way to describe the graceful, yet predatory, way he moved.

No words were spoken as he and my father stared at each other. Both were evenly matched in size and build, though my dad might've been a bit bulkier. If they squared off, there was no telling who would win. Except I prayed like hell it wouldn't come to that.

Then my dad looked past him to find me. Alessio stepped back to allow my dad entry, and I took off running toward him.

His arms wrapped around me when I slammed into him. He barely rocked from the collision. I lost track of time as he held me and I shuddered.

Finally, I separated from the man who had raised me. He glanced from me to Alessio. I knew he was taking in our damp hair and the clothing I was wearing. Then he scanned every visible area of Alessio's home. There likely wasn't a single detail in the condo he missed.

"Whiskey?" Alessio asked as he held his own glass up and gestured to the others.

"The floor is secure?" my dad asked first.

"I assure you it is," Alessio immediately replied.

My father's callused hand wrapped around mine as he drew me along with him. He took one glass and handed it to me. He lifted the other to sniff it before he took a sip, then he nodded to me.

Alessio let loose a dark chuckle. "Afraid I poisoned it? I assure that's not my M.O."

"Oh, I know what your M.O. is," my dad replied in a

deceptively soft tone. "If I was worried, I wouldn't have given one to my daughter first. I just wondered at your taste."

Confused, I glanced from one to the other. Their calculating gazes locked on each other had me warily sipping from the glass and nearly choking on the instant heavy burn of the potent alcohol.

After a few quiet moments, Dad glanced at me, then returned his attention to Alessio. "Now, I want to know what the hell is going on."

For the briefest blink of an eye, Alessio's poise faltered. Then he appeared to carefully weigh his words before he spoke.

"Nivea's stepmother, Jade, has a hit on her. I have no idea how many she's hired or who they are," he finally said.

Though Alessio had already told me this, hearing it again sent my heart into a thunderous rhythm. The deep gold liquid in my glass shook with the tremble in my hand.

"Why?" I whispered.

"She claims that Nivea killed Justin," Alessio explained, answering my question, but only watching my father.

And that was another blow to my psyche. That anyone in their right mind would think I had killed *anyone*, let alone Justin. It fucked with my head and hurt my heart.

"That's utter bullshit. Who the fuck would believe that shit?" my dad ground out.

Alessio winced but quickly covered it. It didn't go unnoticed by anyone.

My dad rolled his eyes and shook his head with a huff.

"I realize that it's ridiculous." Alessio boldly held my father's gaze.

My dad's penetrating gaze narrowed, then he seemed to relax. He gave Alessio a curt nod.

"I'll take care of her."

I frowned at my dad's words. "I can take care of myself," I muttered. Though in this case, I knew damn well that if it hadn't been for Alessio today, I wouldn't be here having this conversation.

And that was a sobering thought.

The two men gave each other an understanding stare, then my dad turned to me. "That's not what I was referring to, Niv. But there are some things that I don't want touching you."

His reply seemed to have a double meaning as Alessio's expression turned to stone, yet he added, "Agreed."

"Fine. Speak in your little secret man-code. But I need to go home. I have a project I'm in the middle of that I need to have finished," I insisted before I placed my glass forcefully on the bar.

"You already told your mom that you were ahead on that. All I need is a week. She'll be safe here?" My dad arched a brow at Alessio with his last question.

"Of course. I share the condo with my younger brother, Leo, but he's out of the country for a few weeks. His room is at the end of the hall to the right, mine is on the left. The two rooms in the middle each have their own bathrooms. You can choose whichever you prefer. There should be toiletries in both." Alessio explained.

My father's dark-blond eyebrows lifted higher, and I

realized that Alessio had pretty much given away that either I'd showered in his brother's bathroom, or his. With everything else he'd noticed earlier, I'd put money on the fact he knew we'd showered together.

As my blood boiled, my hands curled into fists at my side.

"So that's it? The two of you get to make my decisions for me?" I was referring to both of them now and the fact that Alessio had made the decision for me regarding whether or not I wanted to explore the combustible nature of our coupling.

"Nivea. This is serious business. This isn't the time to throw a tantrum about your freedoms or lack of," my dad snipped. I hated this side of him. The cold and ruthless business side.

"A tantrum?" I gasped in outrage. My mouth opened to spew out my rage, but I snapped it shut. Then I picked up the glass and emptied it in two swallows before I forcefully replaced it with a thunk. I turned on my heel and stormed for the bedrooms Alessio had described. Not caring which one I got, I entered the first door and slammed it behind me.

"Of all the bossy asshole moves," I began my grumbling tirade as I paced. Then I snatched a pillow from the bed and smashed it to my face so I could scream into it.

Feeling marginally better, my shoulders slumped and I crawled onto the bed and ended up drifting off to sleep, plotting the demise of the two controlling bastards in the other room.

Despite my anger, I hoped Alessio would come to my

room after my dad went to bed. When he didn't, a little crack started in the corner of my heart, and I knew I'd been an idiot.

There was no way he fucked me because he was truly attracted to me. Had I thrown myself at him? I ran over everything that had happened, but so much of what happened before his mouth was on me was a blur.

However, I knew I hadn't imagined the feel of him inside me. Nor had I imagined how he'd ensured my pleasure before his own.

Now if I could forget it, that would be great.

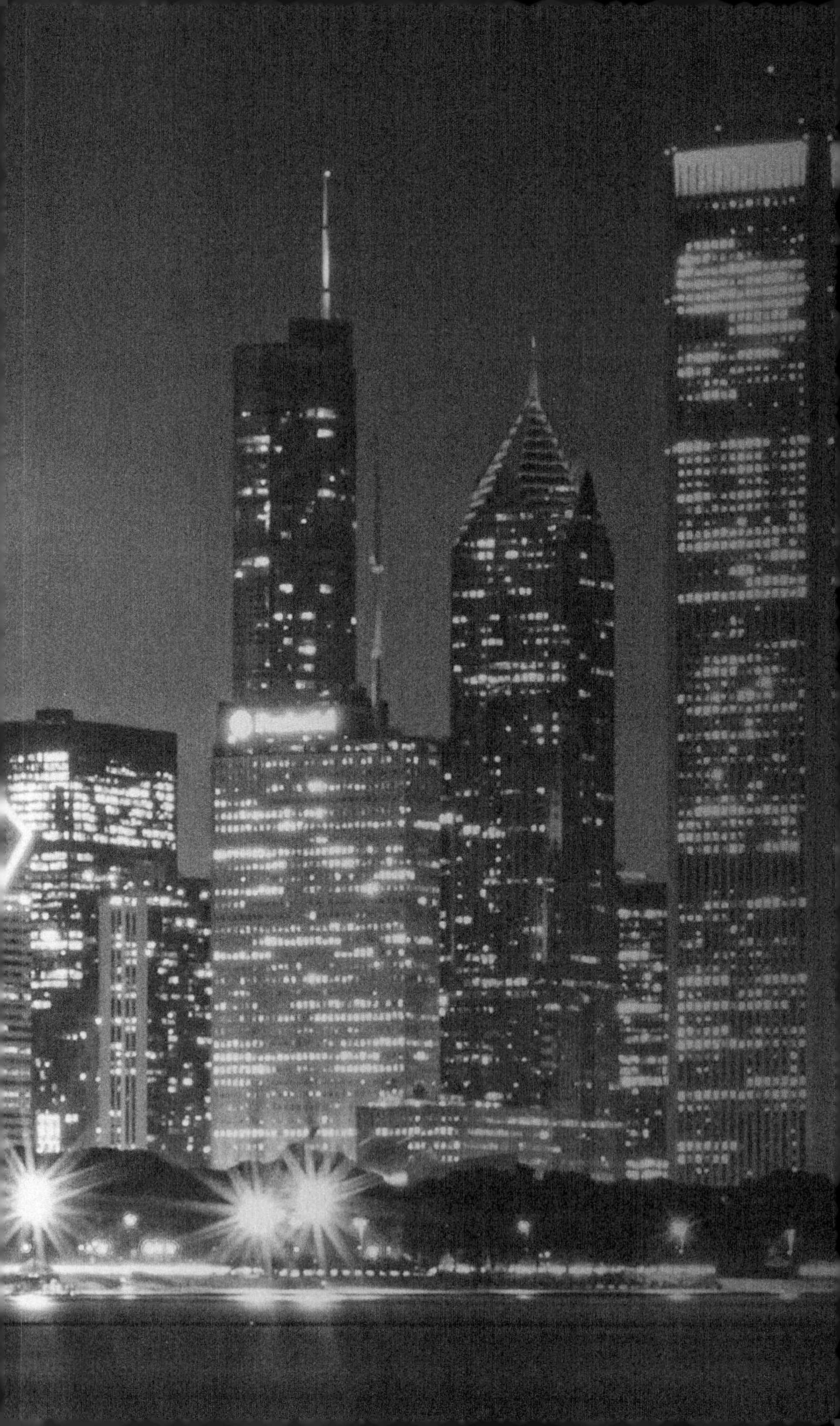

Chapter Six

Alessio

"VITAMIN R (LEADING US ALONG)"—CHEVELLE

"If you take the stepmom out, there's no guarantee the others that she hired won't still finish the job," I told Matthew, though I was pretty sure he already knew that.

"I have no doubt. Which is why I intend to find each and every one of them first."

"You know there's a reason those kinds of deals run through the dark web. Anonymity is a necessary safety precaution," I hedged.

He gave me a cold smile that sent chills down even my own hardened shell.

"You won't be able to find out information like that," I tried again.

"Don't underestimate me and my resources," he smoothly replied.

I huffed a drawn-out breath, then ran a hand through my hair. Then I lifted my drink to take a much-needed swallow.

"When did you start fucking my daughter?"

I choked on the smooth whiskey and covered my mouth as I turned my head away and coughed up what I'd damn near inhaled.

"What?" I croaked.

He leaned his elbows on the bar as he held my gaze. "I'm not an idiot and I haven't stayed alive as long as I have by being unobservant. Did you put your dick in her before or after you decided not to kill her?"

"Jesus. Who the fuck *are* you?" I didn't get rattled easily, but this motherfucker shook me to my damn core.

"Answer the question and I'll answer yours."

Staring into his icy gaze, I clenched my jaw as I debated how exactly to reply. Deep down I knew this wasn't the guy to bullshit. Finally, I bit out my answer. "Tonight was the first time. *After* I protected her."

Like a human lie detector, he searched my gaze for an insanely intense moment. Then he lifted his chin slightly. "I'm mostly retired, but I worked for years as a… paid mercenary."

"You mean an assassin," I drily corrected.

His grin didn't reach his eyes. "Takes one to know one, right?"

"Fuck," I muttered. My brain was rapidly running through my thoughts, clicking on some, discarding others. "Does she know?"

He shrugged. "About you? Obviously not. Me? She has a pretty good idea idea. I sheltered her and her mother from most of it, but there came a time when out of… necessity… they needed to know certain things. I've taught her to be careful and we have protocols in place for a reason. I was afraid living here on her own would make her complacent. I also worried that bitch her biological father married would be an issue—just not to this extent."

"Now what?"

"Now you reach out to your contacts and I reach out to mine. We find out who she hired and we eliminate them and her. How you proceed will determine if you end up on that list," he added the last as casually as one would the weather.

"Meaning?"

"You tell her how you really met her, and I let you live," he calmly stated.

I scoffed. "You realize you're in my home, right? What's to stop me from killing you first?"

"Because, as I said before, that's *my* daughter and I promise you, if I die at your hands, I have conditional responses in place. And I don't think you want to explain to her how you killed her dad." He finished his drink and quietly set the glass down, then pushed back and stood upright.

"How am I supposed to tell her she was my target before I fell for her?" I asked him, bordering on desperation. The fact that I'd admitted I fell for a woman in the span of a few weeks didn't slip my attention. And I also had to admit to myself that I was starting to fall for her before she even knew I existed. Another fucked up part of our situation.

"I'm giving you until the end of the week to tell her the truth," Matt ground out between gritted teeth. "If you can't be honest with her, you don't fucking deserve her. You reach out to who you need to, and I'll reach out to who I need to. We'll talk more in the morning."

With that, he walked off toward my other spare bedroom as if he didn't have a care in the world.

Jesus fucking Christ.

I called Facet the minute Matthew Bulgari retired to his room for the night. After making sure it was a good time, I filled him in on what had transpired.

"Bro, I'm sorry. I was on a job and we had shit for signal. We literally just pulled back into civilization," Facet explained.

"I'm not mad at you, man. I'm just pissed at the situation."

"So… you and the target, huh?" he asked, and I could hear the humor in his voice.

"I didn't say anything about that," I grumbled.

"You didn't need to," he countered. "And I honestly can't believe you're still able to call me—hell, I'm surprised you're alive. That's one bad motherfucker."

"He said he was a paid mercenary."

Facet gave a choking laugh. "That's glossing over it nicely. Matthew Bulgari is—well, was—one of the top assassins in the world. Not to mention, high-risk extractions, and who knows what else. I'm not kidding when I said he's a seriously wicked dude. I cannot believe I didn't look into this one better. I… Jesus fucking Christ, I have no excuses."

"It was a fucked up job all the way around. I shouldn't have agreed to it. We both slipped. The blame doesn't lie on your shoulders alone. Now what?"

We talked for a while longer as we strategized our next moves. By the time I ended the call and went to my room, I was dead on my feet. Except I could smell Nivea everywhere.

And as I dozed off, in my head, I heard those little noises she made as she came.

"I want to go to my loft so I can finish my project," Nivea insisted over coffee.

"No," her father insisted before I could even open my mouth.

"Dad, I'm a grown ass woman," she argued, bright blue eyes flashing like the hottest part of a flame.

"Yes, you are—a grown ass woman with a price on her head," he quietly agreed.

"We don't even know that for sure," she shot back.

"Actually, I know that for a fact," I interjected, immediately realizing I had fucked up.

Her gaze narrowed as her nostrils flared. "How do you know that?"

Matthew cut in. "I've confirmed it."

Though Nivea's skin was pale to begin with, she went positively ashen at his confirmation. She placed her mug on the table with trembling hands.

"I'm supposed to meet with Justin's attorney, too," she murmured as she stared sightlessly at the contents of the mug.

"For what?" Matthew and I both stilled as we watched her closely.

"I don't know."

Matthew and I shared a look. Then he casually tapped

away at his phone before he set it to the side. "I want you to call him back and reschedule for the end of next week."

"So what, I'm just going to live my life in hiding from now on?" Exasperation colored her words.

"No, but this is serious, sweetheart. Just give me a week to see what I can come up with. Please?"

Her shoulders slumped.

"Okay, regardless, I need clothes. I can't keep wearing the same things I arrived in, nor do I want to wear Alessio's clothing."

Ouch. That hurt.

It shouldn't, because she'd already made it glaringly obvious she felt what we did was a mistake. And why was I upset? A beautiful woman had essentially given me amazing sex with no strings. That should make me happy. Ecstatic, even. Yet there was this primitive monster within that wanted to lash out and snarl that she was *mine*.

Fuck. Where did that come from?

"I can go by and get clothing and hygiene items for her," I offered.

Matthew was nodding, but Nivea's once pale face flushed hot pink. "Absolutely not! I don't want you pawing through my… clothes. I'll get what I need. If you can just drop me off at the front door of my building, I'll pack enough for a week and we can come back."

"Niv—" her dad began.

"No. Non-negotiable," she snapped.

"I can buy you some things to get you by," I told her. After all, I could certainly afford it.

"Thank you, but that's silly. I have plenty of my own things and it's wasteful to buy more just so I don't go home. I live on the top floor, it's not like someone is going to come in through a window," she grumbled.

"I'm not worried about someone going in through a window. I'm worried about who could already be there waiting. There's the little fact that someone is after you and that condo of yours is open almost all the way around it, with a hundred different vantage points." Her dad glared.

"I agree with your father." I knew the layout of her block and I hated that the parking garage alone had a ton of places that were perfect for a sniper to post.

"This is ridiculous," she tried again.

"Niv...." Matthew sighed and his head briefly fell forward. Then he stared at his stubborn daughter before he turned to me. "We go at night. Keep your face averted. No one can know. And Nivea, you are *not* going. If you can't agree to this, then you wear whatever Alessio can scrounge up."

Though I could tell she was ticked off, she nodded.

That night, I had Vittorio and Kendall come across the hall to my place to stay with Nivea. After introductions, Matthew and I left dressed casually in jeans, hoodies, and jackets. Thankfully, since it was winter, no one looked strangely at us for having the hoods up as we stepped into the stairwell that we had to have badge access to enter.

We were avoiding the elevator because, according to Matthew, there were cameras in it.

"I can't believe she would want to live here with so little security up front," I muttered.

"Oh, her condo itself has plenty of security. Trust me on that. And she wanted to live in this old building for some unearthly reason," Matthew replied. "Her mother and I bought out the entire floor and had it converted into one large, loft living space. I'm not gonna lie, I would've preferred to get her a place in your building. I'll give you credit, that place is damn near Fort Knox. I'm impressed."

"Thanks." I cocked a brow at him in surprise. With each floor we passed, I noticed each floor had a badge scanner to enter. I was minimally comforted.

We let ourselves into the condo with a code and Matthew disabled the alarm. We left the lights off and worked from the surrounding light that came in through the windows.

"If there is this level of security to get up here, how did someone get into her condo to send emails from her laptop?" I asked as I gazed at the laptop sitting on the kitchen counter. Seeing it had reminded me of that.

Matthew froze in place. Then he slowly spun to face me. "What?"

I explained to him about the emails and what Facet had uncovered without naming my friend.

"You're sure?" he asked, brow furrowed with concern.

"Positive."

Without another word, he silently began checking the condo. I followed suit. It wasn't hard since, other than the bedroom and bathroom, the place was wide open with the occasional support poles. I'd watched her condo from across the road, but I'd never been inside.

When we were satisfied everything was clear, Matthew

used a kitchen trash bag to scoop up the computer. Then he went into Nivea's bedroom and packed a bag. He shoved the bagged laptop inside and zipped it shut.

"I want you to take her out of town when we get back," he quietly told me as we descended the stairs once again.

"What?" I shot him a confused glance.

"If someone was able to get into her condo, utilize her computer, and she never knew? I don't know what else they might have access to here." We left the building and walked several blocks to where we'd parked the car. We hadn't wanted to use public transportation and get caught on any surveillance cameras, either.

"You just said my place was like Fort Knox," I countered.

"Nothing is infallible," he grunted. "And they may already know she's there." Then he told me to stop at a hardware store. I dropped him off and had to go around the block because, of course, there wasn't a single place to park.

He was coming out when I pulled up again. When he got in, he took a few things out of the bag, but I couldn't tell what he was doing as I drove in the crazy traffic. "Can I ask what you're doing?"

"Making sure if there's a tracker on her laptop that it's unable to send a signal," he mumbled as he worked.

"You're building a jammer?" I asked incredulously.

"Call me MacGyver," he replied with a chuckle.

"Who?"

"Jesus, never mind. You're obviously too young."

"Are you talking about that show that Lucas Till was in?" I asked.

He gave me a deadpan stare as he froze his hands. "No. I was referring to the original one with Richard Dean Anderson."

"Oh."

I heard him mutter "kids."

He must've finished because he carefully opened the plastic around the computer, placed something on it and wrapped it back up.

We made the rest of the trip back to my condo in silence. When I parked, he looked at me. "Do you have a car somewhere else?"

I cocked a brow, but didn't reply.

"Good, kid. This is the plan," he told me his idea, and I agreed, as it had merit. I didn't like him referring to me as a "kid."

"She's not going to be happy about it," I muttered as we went up my private elevator.

"I'm aware. I'm also trusting you with the safety of my daughter. Don't make me regret it. Also, remember what I said—one week." His narrowed-eyed gaze held on me until I nodded.

"Roger that," I said.

"Please tell me you used a condom with my daughter," he nonchalantly murmured as the elevator rose.

Without looking at him, I pressed my lips flat.

"I swear to Christ, if you gave her anything, I will cut off your balls and feed them to you," he whispered as the doors slid open on my floor.

At the entrance to my condo, I stopped in my tracks

Blood TIES

and stared at him. "And I would let you. That's how confident I am."

I could've been wrong, but I thought he might've chuckled as I turned my back to him and went inside.

When I heard Nivea moan in pleasure, my spine stiffened. I stalked to the kitchen, then blinked at what I saw.

Kendall, Alia, and Nivea were eating cupcakes and they all froze with pink and purple frosting on their lips. "Hi Alessio," Kendall mumbled over her mouthful of cake and frosting as she waved.

That's when I saw Vittorio and Gabriel sitting at the breakfast bar eating their own cupcakes. They gave me a chin lift as if it was perfectly normal for them to be sitting in my condo eating pink fucking desserts.

"What the hell is going on in here?"

"Kennall mae cub-cooks," Nivea explained as she worked to swallow the ridiculously massive bite of cupcake.

"Any extras?" Matthew asked as he moved around me.

Kendall gestured to the container on the counter. He helped himself.

All I could do was stand there with my mouth parted as my brothers, their women, Nivea, and her father stuffed their faces. Like someone wasn't trying to kill my woman.

My head jerked back at that thought.

No.

Nivea wasn't *my woman*.

I didn't have women that I claimed, I had women I fucked.

Liar, because you knew she was yours the minute you saw her. A little voice whispered in my head.

Once Matthew was licking the last of his frosting from his fingers, he told Nivea, and the rest of my family, the plan.

Nivea went to the bathroom, and I glanced Matthew's way. "Matthew," I began.

"Matt," he corrected.

"Matt. What if Jade didn't kill Justin either?" I asked.

"I don't care. She hired you to kill my daughter. She signed her death warrant with that. Problem?"

"Absolutely not."

"Good."

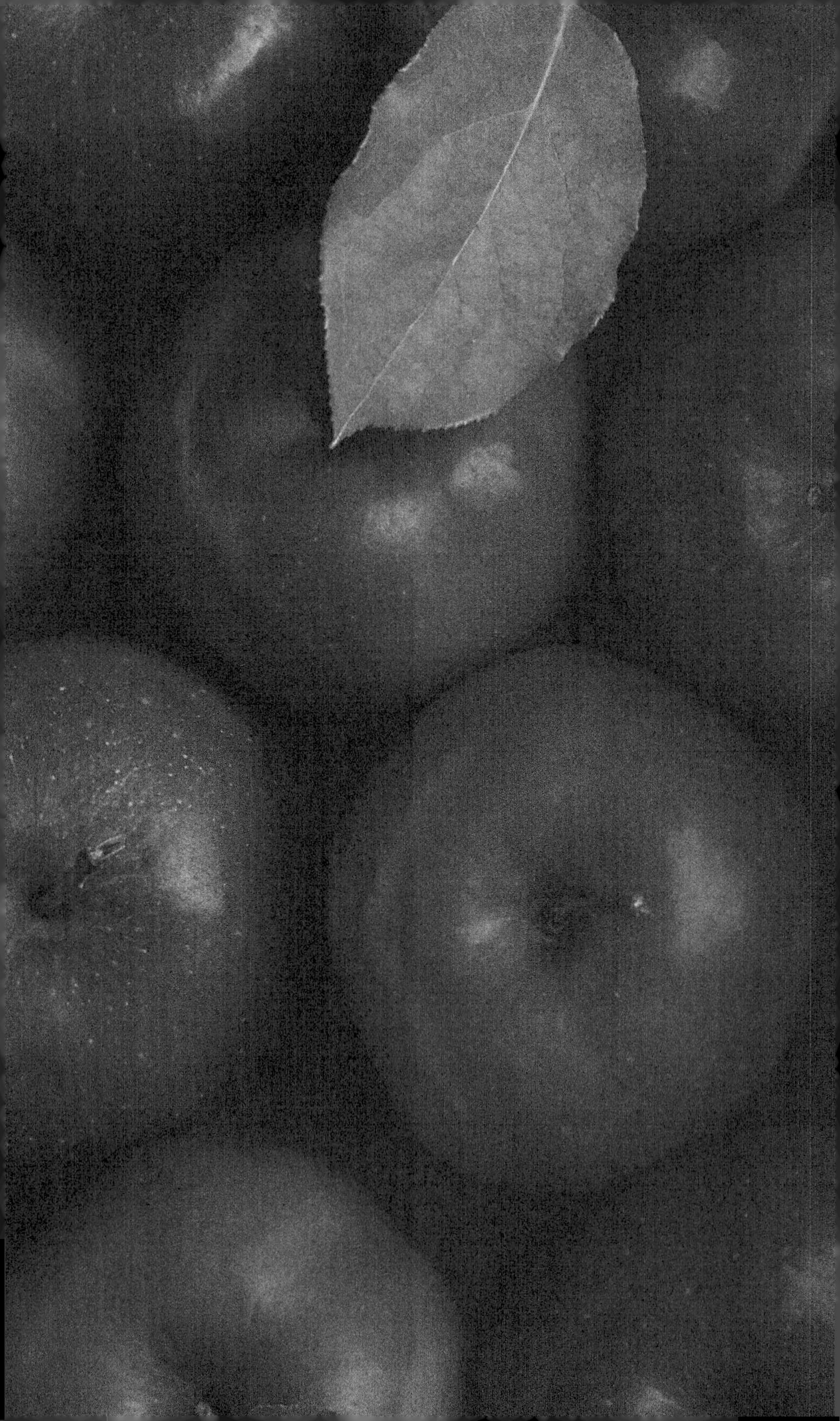

Chapter Seven

Nivea

"WHY'D YOU ONLY CALL ME WHEN YOU'RE HIGH?"—
ARCTIC MONKEYS

When we left Alessio's condo, he was wearing my dad's hoodie and jacket and I was wearing his. My hair was pulled back so none escaped the hood. When we got down to the underground parking, we got in one of Alessio's vehicles and I hid in the backseat. That way, as we pulled out, he appeared to be driving alone.

We drove across town and into a nicer neighborhood, where we pulled into the attached garage of a house. Then we switched to another vehicle. That process was repeated again before I was allowed to sit up in the front seat.

By the time we pulled into a garage of a smaller house in the suburbs, it was nearing dawn. "We'll be staying here."

We went inside.

"So how long do we need to be here?" I asked as I dropped my bag to the floor and my ass to the bed. Alessio was standing in the doorway. What I really want to ask was if he was sleeping with me.

"We'll be here long enough to get some sleep. Then we'll be leaving for my brother's house on Lake Geneva."

"Oh. Okay."

"Is there anything else you need?" He cocked that dark brow and my stomach fluttered.

Feeling bold, I asked, "Where are you sleeping?"

He took a breath and opened his mouth, then he snapped it shut. For several heartbeats, he simply stared at me. Then he exhaled heavily. "I don't think it would be wise for me to sleep in here with you. Neither of us would get much sleep."

Then he turned on his heel, closed the door, and left. I heard another one down the hall open and close. My shoulders slumped. I shouldn't be surprised, but I was hoping after what he'd said earlier, that maybe he couldn't resist me. Yes, I'd been the one to say my dad didn't need to know about what we'd done, but damn, I wished he'd fought me on it. Just a little.

Wait. Was he saying if he stayed in my room, we wouldn't get much sleep because we'd be busy doing other things? My heart fluttered and my stomach rippled and flipped.

"I don't think I'll be getting much sleep anyway," I grumbled as I pulled out my iPad mini and downloaded a new book. I would rather get no sleep because I was busy doing fun things—naked. My book was a close second. Without changing, I curled up on the bed in the nondescript room and stared into space.

Then I started to read. Except the words kept blurring. Despite feeling like I'd be awake all night, my eyes grew heavy, and I was out before I knew it.

It seemed like it was only thirty minutes later when I was being gently shaken.

"Niv, it's time for us to go."

"MmMm," I grumbled as I fought leaving my delicious dream where Alessio was doing everything he'd done to me before, and more. If dreams were rated, this one was definitely an X. Maybe triple.

"Nivea. We have to get on the road."

My eyes popped open because that was not dream Alessio talking to me. I bolted upright and realized I had drool that trailed from my mouth to the pillow. Using the back of my hand, I wiped it away.

"Okay. Yeah. I'm up."

He smirked and I'm pretty sure he laughed at me. I scowled.

"Come on, Snow White. It's time to wake up."

"Don't you mean Sleeping Beauty?" I muttered.

"Definitely Snow White," he murmured as he brushed my hair out of my face with a gentle touch.

It was on the tip of my tongue to ask if he had kissed me to wake me up from my slumber.

Before I was fully awake, I had a cup of coffee in my hand. I frowned at the cup after I tasted it. "How did you know how I like my coffee?"

"I pay attention."

Then we winked and walked out of the room.

My jaw dropped because if he was referring to the day we met at the coffee shop, that was two weeks ago. The coffee was hot as Hades so I decided to let it cool while I washed up and changed clothes. I found my iPad buried in the bedding and put it away.

Using the bathroom across the hall, I washed my face and brushed my teeth. Dragging ass, I packed my belongings up again, grabbed my coffee, and brought my bag out to the kitchen.

"Do you want a bagel?" he asked, holding one up and waving it back and forth.

"Please," I practically moaned. I was damn starving.

"Cream cheese?"

"Just butter."

Once the toaster popped, he prepared both bagels and set a small plate in front of me.

"So who does the dishes?" I asked around a big bite.

"We can flip for it," he replied, and my eyes went wide.

"I was kidding. You made breakfast so I'll do dishes." I smirked.

His bark of laughter was the first time I'd really heard him laugh in days. "I utilized a toaster—that's hardly cooking."

"Hey, it's food and it's morning. That's breakfast in my book."

"Eat."

Didn't need to tell me twice.

We both ended up washing the few items we dirtied. It didn't take long. I was returning everything to its proper place when his phone rang.

"Yes." His short staccato greeting had me glancing his way.

I couldn't be certain, but it sounded like my dad on the other end. A frown tugged at my brow that matched his.

"Get your bag. Now," he demanded as he snagged his keys and we were rushing out into the garage. He tossed his in the backseat of the vehicle that had been waiting in the garage when we arrived. When he tugged mine from my hand and gestured for me to get in, I immediately obeyed. "I'll keep you updated," he said before he ended the call, cursing under his breath.

The garage door was rolling up when he started the car. "Duck down," he told me.

With my head to my knees, I stared at his profile. "Was that my dad?"

"Yes. Change of plans. We're not going to my brother's lake home." He slid on a pair of sunglasses and tossed on a backwards baseball cap.

"Where are we going then? What happened? What did he say?"

"They know where we are and likely where we're going."

"Who?" I asked, exasperated as hell.

"I wish I knew."

There was something he wasn't telling me. "I want to talk to my dad."

"He's indisposed at the moment. We'll call him when we stop."

"Indisposed? What the hell does that mean?" I knew my dad had done some sketchy shit as a mercenary, though he kept the details to himself. Him being "indisposed" sent my anxiety skyrocketing, especially since a few years ago, he told me and Mom he was retired.

At first, Alessio didn't answer me, and I noticed he was glancing frequently in the rearview mirror.

"He's trying to find out who, but his information is… limited… at the moment. I have some friends that I think can help us out. But my friend is very private. He doesn't like discussing a lot of things over the phone." His vague answers were driving me batshit crazy.

"For fuck's sake, Alessio. I've been shot at, chased across Chicago, my loft has been broken into, my private space violated. I think I deserve to know what the fuck is going on! And can I sit up?" By that time, I was shouting at him.

"Give me about five more minutes."

"Ugh!" I grunted in frustration.

"You're good now. We'll be swapping out this car, then heading to a place I know. We're going to take a roundabout route, and we'll swap cars again once we cross the Iowa state line."

"Jesus, how many damn cars do you have?" My eyes bugged as I sat up and glanced out of the window.

"A few. My family has a few more." He checked the rearview again.

I snorted in disbelief. "A *few*?"

He casually shrugged like having multiple residences and twice as many vehicles was a common occurrence. Sure, if his condo was any indicator, he had money. Oh, who was I kidding? I knew damn well his family had money—but for a moment I'd forgotten who his family was.

My eyes rolled.

"So are we just passing through Iowa? Or is that our destination?"

"That's our destination."

"Oh, great, I get to know something," I sarcastically muttered to myself.

We didn't just switch vehicles once before leaving Illinois. Oh, no. We stayed a night in a sketchy as fuck motel, then went south for a while where we picked up a truck. Then we drove west for a while.

That night we stayed in a cabin that was one of those tiny house things outside of Bloomington. I crashed on the small bed, and Alessio took the couch. The next morning, we pulled another truck out of an old barn that I swear looked like it was going to fall over, but the inside seemed to have new lumber framing it.

"Your family must be the most paranoid people I've ever met," I grumbled as we drove away from the cabin.

"That place is mine," he absently replied. I wasn't in the mood to push for conversation because by then I was on the verge of exhaustion. I hadn't had a good night's sleep in days.

The last house was well near the tiny town of Hillsdale. Alessio made a phone call, presumably to my dad—no, I still didn't get to talk to him. We stayed there until it got dark. While we waited, dinner was a couple of frozen pot pies he popped in the oven.

I'd tried to get him to talk, but he only replied with one-word or brief answers.

As we sped down the interstate, he was quiet. All I could

do was watch the miles go by in the dark. As we traveled down I-88, we passed several towns, some small, some bigger, until we got on I-80, where we crossed the Mississippi River and then we were into Iowa.

At the first rest area across the border, we pulled in and parked next to a red Camaro.

"Let's go inside."

"Oh! He speaks!"

Leaning his forearm on the steering wheel, he turned to face me. A deadpan expression met my gaze. "Sarcasm is the lowest form of wit."

I stuck my tongue out at him and flung the door open. He caught up to me as I neared the building.

"And that was a level of maturity that was unnecessary." Steam puffed away from his mouth as he spoke.

A middle finger was my reply to that before I sped up to get out of the cold. I wasn't for certain, but I think the bastard laughed.

Once inside, I spun to face him. "Now what?"

"Do you have to go to the bathroom? We won't be stopping again for a couple of hours at least."

I huffed out a breath through my nose. Then I maturely stomped into the bathroom and took care of my business. When I exited, he was waiting.

"Ready?"

"As I'll ever be."

"Follow along."

"Umm, okay?"

He placed my hand in the crook of his elbow and leaned over to kiss my cheek as he gazed lovingly at me.

I cocked a brow, and he brought his lips to my ear. "That's not playing along."

Of their own volition, my eyes rolled. Not. Maybe that's why I didn't realize that the door he opened for me was cherry-red. As he helped me in, I quietly squeaked, "Who's car is this?"

"Leo's." He was backing out of the parking spot by then.

"Who?"

"My younger brother."

"What about our bags?" I asked as I turned in my seat to look at the car we left behind.

"They're in the trunk already."

"Like by magic?" I pursed my lips at him.

"Oh, the sarcasm is strong with you today."

"Guess I'm not very witty," I drolly replied.

After that, whenever I tried to engage him in conversation, he remained silent or I got the one-word grunted answers. The entire time, he was watching that rearview mirror.

"You never told me. Where, exactly, are we going?" I asked for about the millionth time as I watched out the window. There was a lot of nothing that we went past and after about all I could stand of utter silence, I spoke.

"I told you. A friend's place."

"Vague much?" I huffed.

"You don't know them."

"No shit." I rolled my eyes. This was not the man that

had fucked my socks off several nights ago. Hell, by now, I pretty much lost track of time.

It was almost midnight, and I was tired, cranky, and hungry. True to his word, we hadn't stopped once since the rest stop. "I need to pee."

He sighed. "Can it wait another forty-five minutes?"

"No."

He grumbled under his breath, but he got off at the next exit that said there was a gas station. "Stay in the car."

I rolled my eyes. He efficiently got gas, then came around to my door. When he opened it, he held his hand out, and I almost spitefully ignored it, but I was stiff and not in the mood for a fight.

He firmly held my upper arm as we walked inside the older building.

"Bathroom?" He asked the woman behind the counter who had been doing something on her phone.

She grabbed a key hooked to a flyswatter and handed it to him without looking away from her phone. "It's outside, around back," she told us, still without making eye contact.

Together, we made our way around, following the signs. When we got to the chipped and rusting door, I curled my nose.

"Beggars can't be choosers," he chided.

Was that a smile I heard in his tone?

When he unlocked the door, I stepped in. It smelled like mothballs, but it seemed clean at least. The door shut, and I turned, letting out a squeak of surprise. "What are you doing in here?"

"I'm not leaving you alone."

"There's no one in here but me! And there aren't any windows!" I squawked.

"Not taking chances. Your father was explicit in his instructions that I not let you out of my sight for anything."

"Well, at least turn around," I sputtered.

He gave me a smirk that, with my bladder about to burst and his nearly mute behavior for the last several hours, shouldn't make me clench at the apex of my thighs. We were in a rundown public bathroom for fuck's sake!

"Not like I haven't seen it," he purred.

My eyes narrowed as I glared. He chuckled, but thankfully turned around.

"This is ridiculous," I muttered as I quickly dropped my pants and carefully placed toilet paper over the seat. I was *not* sitting on a public restroom seat.

I hurried, and he made sure to go outside first before he waved me out.

When we returned the key, the chick behind the counter took it from us and still didn't make eye contact. "Hard to get good help these days," Alessio muttered.

Back on the highway, we followed it until we hit Ankeny. The sign as we exited said North East 14th Street/69 and we took it north out of town.

More expanses of nothing passed until we pulled into what looked like the driveway to a business of some kind. Strange that a business would be out in the middle of the country.

Flood lights on the corners lit up the parking area. There

was a big metal building with motorcycles parked out front. What looked like several smaller buildings surrounded that one, and across a field there was a big farm.

At the entrance, a young guy with a scraggly beard stopped us. Before the guy could ask, Alessio told him, "We're here to see Facet."

"And you are?"

"The Huntsman. He'll know who I am if you tell him that."

The Huntsman?

The guy stepped back a few feet and used a small walkie talkie. The next thing I knew, he was opening the gate and waving us through. We parked at the end of a bunch of bikes. I couldn't believe that many people would be out on motorcycles in this cold.

We got out and I warily scanned the area. The walk-through door to the massive building swung open and a guy with a dark mop of hair that fell over one eye stepped out.

"Hey brother, what's up?" the dark-haired guy asked as he gave Alessio some sort of handshake-hug combination. As he did, he cast an assessing glance my way.

"Facet, I'm sorry we're just dropping by. Ordinarily, I would've given you a heads up, but it's complicated," Alessio explained before he and the man had a seemingly unspoken conversation.

Dropping by, like we had driven across town instead of a state away. I snorted and they both faced me. Several other scary-looking guys ambled out of the building. A broad-shouldered, older man with a salt and pepper beard broke away from the rest and approached.

"Venom, it's good to see you again," Alessio offered as they did the same bro-hug gesture. "This is Nivea," he finally introduced.

"Hello, Nivea. It's nice to meet you," Venom said as he held out a big, thick hand.

Hoping his name wasn't indicative of what could happen by simply touching him, I swallowed hard and placed my hand in his. We shook and he gave me a small, but friendly, smile.

"You, too," I mumbled.

Introductions followed, and names got thrown at me that I wouldn't possibly remember. Though the guys had all seemed pretty scary at first, I realized they were pretty friendly, and truthfully, a good-looking bunch. Well, in that bad-boy sort of way.

"Do you have somewhere Nivea can freshen up and rest for a bit? And I'll explain why we're here." Alessio addressed Venom.

"Of course. Voodoo, would you show her to your old room?" he asked one of them. The man I now remembered introducing himself as Voodoo stepped forward, and I was struck speechless by his icy gaze. Something cold bumped my hand and I jumped as I looked down.

"That's Zaka," Voodoo explained with a quirk at the corner of his mouth. The giant black dog nudged my hand again and I scratched behind his ears. "He obviously likes you. Follow me, I'll show you where you can get cleaned up."

I followed him and Zaka into the massive metal building.

At the far end, it was two stories high, and the main end had what looked like a living room area with a couple of huge TVs, and I was pretty sure—a stripper pole. Music blared out of big speakers mounted high on the walls.

A bunch of people were hanging out at that end. All of them glanced our way as we came in. Their attention followed us as we went the opposite direction. I couldn't have said if they were guys, girls, or a mixture because I kept my eyes on the scary, pretty man and his equally beautiful dog.

We passed a decent-sized bar with what looked like a kitchen behind it. In front of it, there were a bunch of mismatched tables we walked through before we went into a short hall underneath a set of stairs.

"In here," Voodoo instructed as he opened a door. "There's a bathroom through there." He pointed. "There might be some T-shirts and basketball shorts in the closet, and the bedding is clean if you want to hit the hay."

"Thank you, I think I will."

"Oh, and the WiFi info is on a paper taped in the desk drawer," he mentioned as he pointed at the small desk in the corner.

"Thanks again."

The minute he left, I took a quick shower, pulled on the clothes he'd mentioned—after I smelled them to see if they were indeed clean. Making a mental note to ask Alessio to call my dad, I crawled between the sheets and I couldn't keep my eyes open.

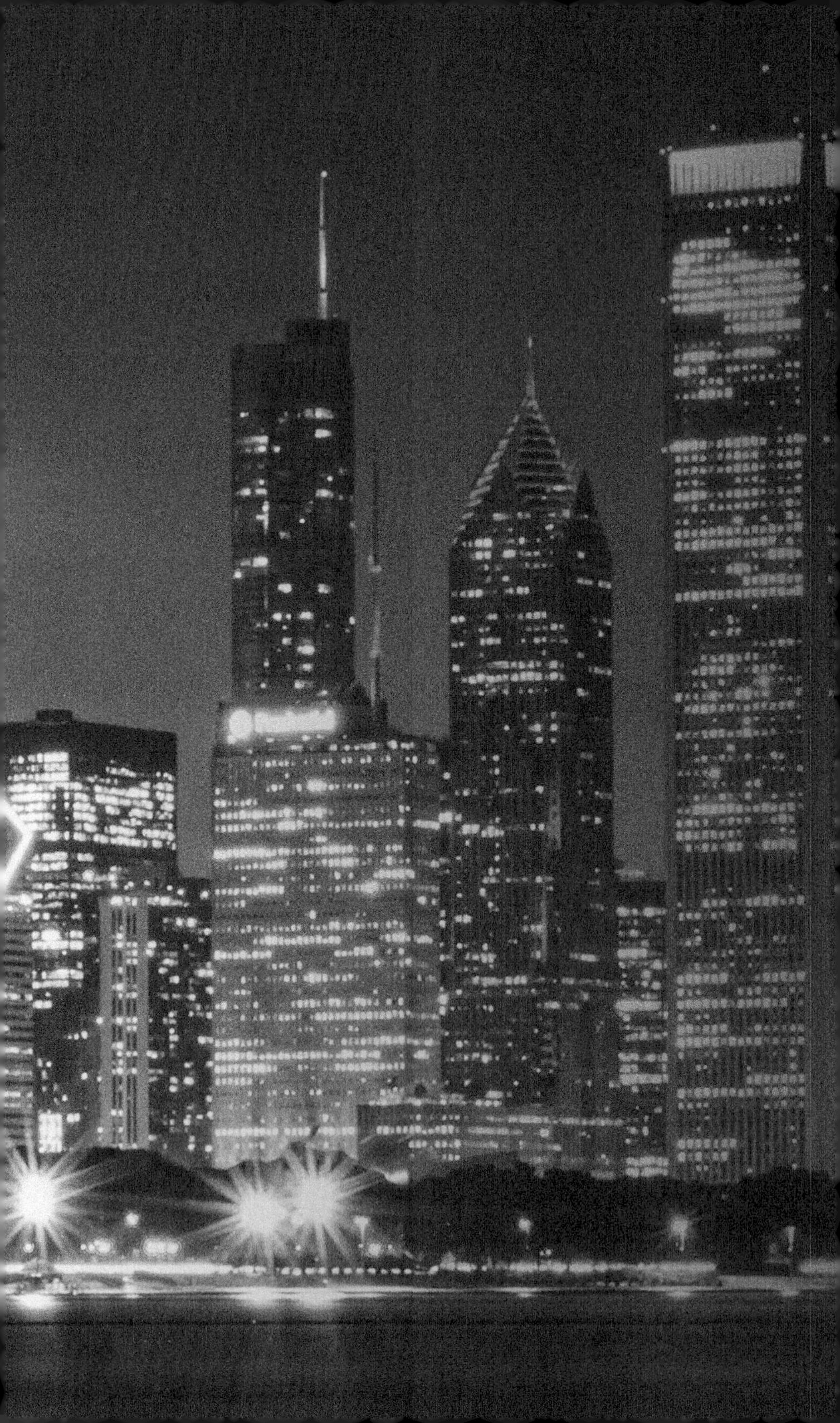

Chapter EIGHT

Alessio

"MAKE UP SEX"—MACHINE GUN KELLY AND BLACKBEAR

Once Voodoo brought Nivea inside, I followed Venom and Facet into the conference room they used for their meetings they called "church." We took a seat at their table. A few minutes later, Hawk joined us.

"What's going on?" Venom asked, cutting right to the chase once Hawk was seated.

A humorless laugh escaped me. "Don't think it's just a friendly visit?"

Venom cocked a brow at me and drew his chin back a bit. His actions told me he knew better.

My chuckle was humorless as I shook my head. "Sorry, I'm in the middle of an absolute shitshow."

I explained everything from when I took the job until that moment. I ended with, "So here we are."

"Christ, I can't believe the stepmom is trying to frame your girl for murder."

I didn't correct his assumption that Nivea was my girl,

but neither did I confirm it. The last several days of being with her had taxed my self-control to the limit.

"Frame her? No. She's going straight for the jugular. For some reason, she put that hit out on Nivea. I'm pretty sure I know why, but I don't have the proof. That's where Facet will come in." I motioned to Facet before I continued.

"I think when it took me longer than she expected, she hired someone else. Whoever it is, they're good. They've been on my ass the whole time. That's why I decided to come here—her dad wanted her out of Chicago. Initially, we were headed up to my brother's lake house. Somehow, the other guy knew that's where we were going and was waiting for us there." I shook my head.

"How do you know he was there waiting, if you changed your plans and came here?" Venom rested his forearms on the edge of the table and folded his hands.

"Because Matthew Bulgari is her father," I reiterated.

"That is one bad motherfucker, Prez," Facet confirmed.

"You know him?" Venom asked Facet, who shook his head.

"Not personally, no. But word gets around. If you know, you know, and trust me when I tell you, *I know*. I had an associate who worked with him on a job. It was right after I got out of the army—before I came here. The stories he told made even me nervous. Matt Bulgari's got some insane connections," Facet explained.

"Better than yours?" Venom asked Facet with a raised brow.

"Yes," Facet replied.

Venom rubbed a hand over his mouth as he considered everything.

"What's the motive? Did the biological father change his will, leaving the money to the daughter?"

"Nivea."

"What?" Venom looked over at me in confusion.

"Her name is Nivea—the daughter," I clarified.

Venom shot me a calculating look. The corner of his mouth twitched, and he gave me a subtle nod. "Did the biological father leave his money to Nivea? Maybe that's the motive," he corrected.

I glanced at Facet in question.

"Well, you'd be pretty spot on. I hacked into the attorney's computer and it turns out, about two months ago, Justin changed his will. It now specifies that, upon his death, if it was a result of natural causes, his fortune gets divided between several charities, his wife, and any living, natural-born children—but everything stays in trust for five years." Though he was explaining everything, Facet's fingers were obviously flying over his keyboard because all I could hear was the rapid clicking of the keys.

"For *five years*? Who does that?" I frowned, running a frustrated hand through my hair.

"Someone who is afraid he'll be killed for his money?" Hawk chimed in with a shrug.

"Makes sense," Venom agreed as he slowly stroked his graying beard.

"And another interesting thing I found in the attorney's files was that he also made the arrangements for his cremation the week before his death." Facet was as stumped as I was by the strange series of events.

"What if the stepmom—what was her name again?" Venom asked.

"Jade," I replied.

"Who's to say Jade didn't forge those documents? It's pretty convenient that he requests immediate cremation a week before he dies. Or am I an absolute moron?" Venom's tone began to border on exasperated.

"I thought about that too. Trust me, I've been scouring this shit left and right. You're absolutely correct, the one with the most motive is Jade. She signed a prenuptial agreement prior to the marriage. The will gives her a big chunk, whereas with the prenup, she got a flat million." Facet strummed his fingers on the table.

"Christ, how much was Justin worth if a million isn't enough for her?" Venom asks with a look of surprise.

Facet lifted his dark gray eyes and met everyone's questioning stares. "Billions."

"Fuck," Hawk muttered.

"Then it would make sense that Jade killed Justin. With the cremation request, if she poisoned him, but made it look like a heart attack or something, the body was incinerated so she could conveniently hide the evidence. Can you find out who notarized the cremation request? Or anything that would show she might have forged shit?" Venom asked Facet.

"I'm trying to pull up the scanned documents." Facet was focused on his screen as he typed away.

Venom, Hawk, and I waited impatiently.

"Bad news, guys." Facet looked up. "There was an autopsy done. According to the report, cause of death is ruled cardiac arrest. Also, both the new will and the request for cremation were signed in the law firm's office, witnessed by Justin's personal assistant, and notarized by the firm's notary."

"There are a lot of things that can be done that end up being ruled cardiac arrest. That's not as concerning to me as the sudden change in his funeral arrangements. You think she could've played with shit that much? Or maybe Justin was getting some kind of early dementia or something. Is that possible?" I asked, beginning to get frustrated and needing answers.

"I'll tell you what—if you give me a few hours, I can probably get into the security feeds for the attorney's office to see if Justin went in there the day it was signed," Facet offered.

"You do that, I'm ready to go home. Message me if you find anything. Until then, you're safe here. Get some rest," Venom encouraged me, then sighed. "God knows, I'm done hanging out here. I just have to see if Loralei is ready to go home."

Venom stood up, as did Hawk. I got to my feet with them and shook their hands. "I appreciate you letting us stay here for a bit."

"Anytime, Alessio. We have a history and Facet speaks highly of you. To me, that makes you family." Venom gripped my shoulder before giving it a firm pat. "I'll see you tomorrow. I'll let Squirrel know that if there's anything you need, he can run to town for you. If you want, I can park your car in one of the outbuildings to keep it out of sight. That's a pretty noticeable and memorable ride you have out there."

"That would be great. Thanks," I said with a tired smile. It was crazy that a bunch of bikers were more like family than my grandfather had ever been. I wasn't overly close to my dad either. Gabriel and Vittorio spent more time with him learning the ropes. I had no interest in having anything to do with what my grandfather believed was his legacy. Fuck that and fuck him.

Venom and Hawk left the room. Facet and I remained.

"Do you think you can dig into who the guy on our ass is?" I asked Facet, leaning forward with my elbows on the table. It's a long shot, but it's worth asking.

"I can try, but you know as well as I do that there's a reason that shit is done on the dark web. Would you want any old hacker like me finding you and who your targets have been?" He cocked a brow as he tilted his head.

"Yeah, I get it. But I know you have your ways." It was the first time I'd openly acknowledged that I knew there was more to Facet than met the eye. He played the part of computer nerd very well. But there was a reason he was in this chapter of the RBMC. The fact that they had… gifts… was a well-guarded secret, but my brothers and I had been part of their trusted inner circle for some time now.

Facet lifted his chin as he eyed me warily. "I'm a warlock, not a magician," he drily replied. Except his dark eyes seemed to flicker with silver. Then he blinked and it was gone.

I smirked. "Sure."

"I'll see what I can do," he conceded.

At that, I sobered. "Thank you—for doing this and for being my friend. You're probably the only one I have."

"That's not true. Any one of my brothers would be there for you."

"Maybe. But it doesn't mean I'd trust them with the things I trust you with."

The corner of his mouth kicked up before he gathered his laptop, and we left the room. He pointed out which room I was using for the night and went on his way.

With a sigh, I turned the knob and went inside. Then I froze. Lying in the bed, with the covers draping the luscious curve of her hips, was my greatest temptation. My jeans grew tight and my zipper began to bite into my rapidly growing dick. I turned on my heel and stepped back into the hall.

Squirrel was coming out of the room across from me. He was shirtless and his hair was messed up—like someone's hands had been all through it.

"Hey, by chance, is there another room?" I quietly asked him.

"Sorry, but no. We have a bunch of brothers visiting from out west. Voodoo's room is the only one free right now," he explained with an apologetic wince.

"Shit," I muttered.

"Problem I can help with?"

"I didn't realize they put me and Niv in the same room," I grumbled, trying not to sound ungrateful.

"I thought she was with you," he observed with a confused pinch between his brows.

"Not exactly," I hedged, running my hand over my mouth. My damn cock was quite happy to go back in the room and was screaming at me to do so immediately.

Which was why I knew it was a bad idea. Her dad might kill me. Yes, we'd already fucked, but that was adrenaline. It was a terrible idea for me to give into that again, because there was something about her that was different than other women and that was dangerous for so many reasons.

Yet, here we were and unless I wanted to sleep on the floor, I would be stuck sharing the bed with her. Bad fucking idea, but I wasn't taking the damn concrete floor.

Buying myself some time and doing my best to steel my resolve, I used the bathroom and got ready for bed. In my boxers, I climbed into the bed. Staring at the ceiling, I tried to ignore the scent of her perfume on the pillow. Or maybe that was coming from her hair. Either way, it was drawing me in and I gritted my teeth to fight the pull.

But then, she rolled over.

She snuggled into my side and threw one leg over mine. As she adjusted herself in her sleep, my shoulder became her pillow and one hand rested over my pounding heart. Her damn tits were smashed against my side, and I could feel the heat of her pussy through her panties.

Fuck, I wanted nothing more than to roll her over and do dirty, dirty things to her.

Silently, I bit my lip, and internally, I groaned. My fingers twitched with the desire to touch her. Losing the battle, I reached up and sifted my fingers through her silky black hair. Then I wrapped my other hand around hers that still rested on my chest.

"Alessio?" Her voice was husky from sleep and only made things worse.

"They didn't have any other rooms. I planned to stay on my side of the bed," I stiffly announced.

She pushed up to her elbow, forcing me to release her hair and allowing her dark tresses to spill around her shoulders as she stared down at me. "Why?"

"Why what?" I played stupid to buy myself time to get my shit under control.

"Why would you want another room?" The hurt in her tone hit me in the chest.

"Jesus, Niv, I'm trying to do the right thing here," I groaned as I threw one arm over my eyes. There would be time to figure out what the strange pull she had on me was after we got out of this mess. Until then, I needed to stay strong and be a good man for the first time in my life.

Her hand wrapping around my shaft had me sucking in a sharp breath. I wanted to push into her hand, seeking blissful friction. It didn't matter that a layer of fabric separated us. But I held strong.

"Who says it's the right thing?" she whispered, and her breath fanned over my chest.

My eyes popped open as my arm dropped. When her lips brushed across my pec, I practically hissed. Then I almost swallowed my tongue as she slid down and hooked her fingers in the waistband. I kept telling myself I needed to stop her, but hell if I could make the words come out.

Slowly, she pulled them down further, freeing my cock and then gripping it in her hand. I couldn't have stopped the way my shaft throbbed in response if my life depended on it.

"Mmm," she hummed in satisfaction.

"What are you doing?" I choked out, though it was a rhetorical question. Then she lowered her head and licked the clear bead of liquid that was leaking out and my hips surged up of their own volition. "Niv."

Her answer was to lick around the head, then softly wrap her lips around it. She flattened her tongue on the underside as she drew me further into her mouth. The slight scrape of her teeth along the sensitive flesh had me grabbing her hair. When she sucked as she drew back, I wanted to grab her and thrust back in. Each time she did that was a beautiful form of torture.

When I hit the back of her throat, I almost lost my ever loving mind. Each him she repeated her actions, I slipped closer to the edge. Whoever taught her the things she did with her mouth made me want to both thank and kill them at the same time.

It wasn't long before my control disintegrated, and I threaded my hands in her hair and guided her at the pace I needed. Then my spine tingled straight down to my dick and my balls drew up tight. I tried to pull her off, but she growled around me and squeezed the base of my cock. That was my breaking point because I drove deep into her perfect mouth and exploded.

"Fuck woman," I panted as my dick gave one last pulse and a shudder shook me from head to toe.

She lifted her head, sucking hard as she withdrew, resulting in a final burst of pleasure that made me groan.

The grin that curved her plush lips was both wicked

and beautiful. She swiped her thumb over the corner of her mouth and licked it clean.

"Jesus, that was hot," I said between jagged breaths.

"Did it feel like the wrong thing to do?" she asked with a smirk that made her cornflower blue eyes twinkle.

It was my turn to growl as I flipped her to her back and returned the favor.

Then it wasn't long before she threw her head back on the pillow and she came on my tongue. Moaning, I lapped it all up and I was hard as a rock again. She might've still been squeezing my fingers as she slumped back and her legs fell bonelessly wide.

"We need to get some sleep," I told her as I kissed her pretty pussy, then her hip. I moved up her body until we were eye to eye. But went I tried to roll off, she locked her legs around my hips.

My gaze clashed with hers and a shiver shot down my spine and spread to my limbs. Need made my stomach clench. Greed made me want what I really didn't deserve.

Then she whispered three little words that would be my undoing.

"I want you."

"You shouldn't," I replied with regret heavy in my tone.

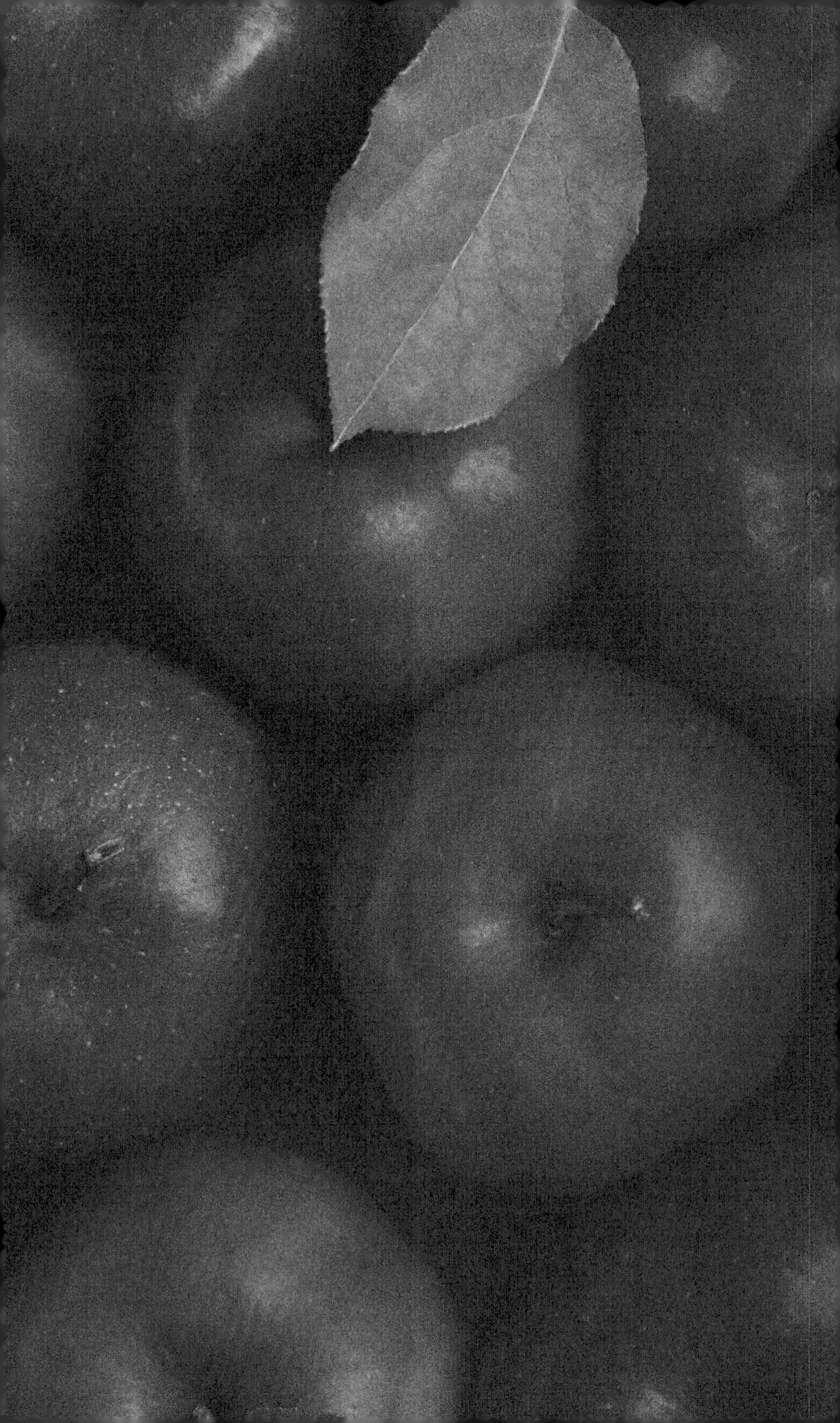

Chapter NINE

Nivea

"SEX, DRUGS, ETC."—BEACH WEATHER

"Are you afraid of my dad?" I asked, but kept my legs hooked around his hips. The way his cock went hard against me told me it wasn't because he wasn't turned on.

He snorted and shook his head. "Your dad has some seriously badass shit going on, but no. Unfortunately, there are few things I'm truly afraid of."

It made me wonder what kinds of things pushed fear through his veins. He was tied up with the mob—that had to come with its fair share of things that would make your blood run cold. No, correction—his family *was* the mob—it wasn't just ties to them.

They were blood ties.

"Then why do you think this is a bad idea? Why do you think I shouldn't want you?"

Bracing his weight on one elbow, he gently toyed with a lock of my hair. His attention was focused on his fingers smoothing over the strands. I wondered if he would answer me.

"Morally, we exist on two different planes. There are things about me you don't know—things I don't *want* you to know. You are everything good and sweet, and I'm… not." He huffed a humorless laugh before giving his head a little shake.

"Why don't you let me be the judge of that?" I reached up to cup his cheek. With gentle pressure, I pressed on his face to make him look at me. Reluctantly, he allowed it.

"Because you wouldn't be making an educated decision," he rebutted. A flash of what seemed to be pain was there in his gaze, but quickly gone.

"Then educate me. Tell me your deepest, darkest secrets and let me come to my own conclusions. You saved me, you can't be all bad," I encouraged with a teasing smile that he didn't return.

"I'm worse than bad, baby. It would be better for all involved that you don't know," he quietly murmured.

"Maybe I like the morally gray boys," I whispered as tilted my hips in a way that aligned the end of his cock with my aching, wet core. With my heels digging into his backside, he started to go in.

"God dammit, Nivea," he groaned in protest. But it was weak because he didn't fight me. As I wiggled to get him deeper, he sucked in a hissed breath, but he gave in. One swift snap of his hips, and he was deeply seated and stretching my pussy in the best way possible.

"Yesss," I hissed as my hands dropped to his shoulders and my nails raked over his skin. My back arched and I knew

I squeezed the fuck out of his cock, because I damn near came at the way he filled me.

He clutched the pillow on either side of my head as he watched me with heavy-lidded eyes. Then he slowly withdrew and plunged back in.

I saw stars.

My body tingled.

He did it again.

And again, and again, and again, until I was screaming his name, and he immediately slapped a hand over my mouth to silence me. Not once during all that did he lose his rhythm. When my cries subsided, he removed it, then pressed a soft kiss to my lips in apology.

He reached one hand down to clutch my ass cheek as he drove in, then his pace quickened and a low moan slipped free. His lips kissed along my skin, pausing only to suck or bite at whim. As he moved along my jaw, he was almost frantic and so was I.

I ground against him with each wild thrust, and though I was shocked, I knew I was going to come again.

When he released his grip on my ass and smoothed his hand up my side, I whimpered. His deft fingers found my nipple and pinched hard. He groaned my name against the sensitive skin below my ear and I moaned. "You're so fucking beautiful," he whispered.

What was crazy, was never in my life had I felt so beautiful with a man. No, more than beautiful—*desirable*. As our bodies continued to come together in a steady rhythm, he tasted everywhere he could reach, and his breaths became uneven as he lifted his head and stared down at me.

I slid a hand up over his shoulder to cup the side of his neck. His pulse pounded under my thumb, and I swear it matched the thundering of my own. Sweat left a sheen over his brow. His pupils were huge, almost swallowing up the stormy blue of his irises. Lost in his gaze, my body began to tense. Pressure gathered and grew.

His white teeth gripped his lower lip and a wildness took over. Gone was the steady, even pace. In its place was a primal, driving need. Skin slapped and my heartbeat whooshed in my ears. The first pulse of his cock, coupled with the tugging and twisting on my nipple, set me off.

"Alessio!" I gasped as the fireworks went off inside me and I clung to him. The ecstasy throbbing through my pussy and spreading through my body sent me careening into a place where all I felt was bliss—and all I saw were the flashes of light behind my eyelids.

All I felt was him pouring everything he had inside me.

After I slowly floated back to reality, my body went limp, but my legs remained hooked around him. His forehead rested on my shoulder as he took a deep, shuddering breath.

"Fuck, Nivea," he whispered in a raspy voice. His weight was comforting, but not suffocating, as we simply existed in each other's space. The muted sounds of music and people laughing filtered into the room and I remembered where we were.

For a few moments, we didn't move. Finally, he lifted his head and stared down at me. So many things were said in the silence, though no words were spoken. He lowered his lips to mine and the kiss he gave me was sweet and gentle.

When he left my body, I whimpered at the loss. He padded to the bathroom and returned with a warm washcloth that he used to clean me up. Then he tossed it into the bathroom where I heard it land in the tub with a splat. He climbed into bed and pulled me close.

"We're gonna figure this out," he softly whispered into my hair. Then we dozed off.

I woke to an empty bed, but I smiled to myself and relished in the ache between my thighs. Feeling lazy and satisfied, I snuggled into the bedding and waited to see if Alessio would return. My growling stomach drove me from the comfort of the bed, and I brushed my teeth, then dressed and wandered out to see if I could find some food.

As I turned the corner, I heard a familiar laugh and froze in my tracks. Then a grin stretched across my face and I ran across the room, oblivious to anyone but the big man getting up from his seat at one of the tables. I threw myself in his arms and he squeezed me tight.

"I'm so glad you're here," I told my dad, who kissed the top of my head.

"I got here as soon as I could," he rumbled, then released me.

That was when I noticed I'd made a spectacle of myself. There were several couples and a few single guys sitting around the surrounding tables. Several of them had plates of food and a growl erupted from my middle.

My dad chuckled. "Let's get you a plate."

I followed him into the kitchen. A redhead in ice-cream cone PJ pants looked up from where she was rinsing dishes, then placing them in the dishwasher. She smiled as she stood upright and faced me. I saw her tank top matched the pants.

"Hi, I'm Willow. There's plenty left," she motioned to several industrial-looking silver pans with foil over them.

"Thanks," my dad told her with a friendly grin and a nod. He showed me where the plates and silverware were, then poured me a glass of OJ. Leave it to my dad to figure out where everything is within minutes of arriving somewhere.

"When did you get here?" I asked the next thing I was wondering out loud.

"Been here about an hour or so," he replied as he poured himself another cup of coffee.

As I filled my plate, I noted he was wearing the black cargo pants, boots, and tight long sleeve shirt I remembered seeing him in occasionally as a child. They never told me the specifics, but when I was old enough, my dad had explained that he'd been a mercenary after getting out of the military. It was why we had so many protocols in place. He never wanted me to be completely unprepared.

Motioning toward them, my gaze narrowed, and I asked, "What's up with all that?"

"Eat and then we'll talk about it."

We joined everyone else. As I took my first bite, Alessio came walking out of the back with the man he'd called Facet.

My cheeks heated and one side of Alessio's mouth lifted into a slight grin.

Alessio dropped into the vacant chair next to me and across from my dad. "Matt," he greeted.

My dad gave him a subtle chin lift. An unspoken conversation seemed to pass between them. My eyes flickered between the two of them as I frowned and my chewing slowed. When neither said anything, I resumed my meal, but kept darting glances their way.

The rest of the people filtered off a few at a time as they finished eating and took their dishes to the kitchen. They broke off in different directions, with several going outside. I heard multiple motorcycles start up and then drive off. After I took my last bite, I started to get up to wash my dishes.

"I've got it," Willow offered as she took it from me. I didn't miss the intense stare that she shared with Facet before her cheeks flushed and she hurried back to the kitchen. Facet watched her walk back with a heated gaze.

Finally, it was only me, Alessio, my dad, and Facet.

"Okay, spill. What the hell is going on?" I directed the question at the three of them, hopeful that one of them would answer me.

"I think things are handled. Just in case, I want you to stay here for a few more days. I'll be sticking around as well. Once we know it's safe, we'll take you back to Chicago," my dad vaguely explained.

"You think? So did you find out who chased me and Alessio?"

Again, there was an exchanged glance, but this time it included Facet as well.

"I'm pretty sure we took care of it," my father said in a tone I hadn't heard in several years until the last few weeks.

"Then I can go home?"

"Not quite yet. Like I said, give us a few days," he repeated. Again, he didn't elaborate.

"So that's it? You said you would explain things after I ate," I grumbled as I crossed my arms in frustration.

"And I did. Explaining things doesn't necessarily mean giving details. You know what you need to know," my dad sternly came back with.

"I'm so sick and tired of people thinking I'm too sensitive or sheltered to be told details. I'm not an idiot, and I'm tougher than I look—you made sure of that. You didn't raise a wimp, Dad," I groused before I stood up and stalked back to the room.

Firmly, I closed the door. Grumbling under my breath, I dug through the small bag we'd gone on the run with and pulled out my iPad. With a huff, I flopped on the bed and started to read. Halfway into the chapter I was reading, there was a knock on the door.

"Yes?" I called out, heart hammering and hoping it wasn't my dad or Alessio. Maybe I'd acted childish, but if they wanted to treat me like a child, I guess they deserved that type of behavior from me. And I was pissed, so I just wanted to be mad for a little while.

When the door opened and Alessio walked in, I sighed.

"Hey," he started as he tucked his hands in the front pockets of his jeans. His brow was furrowed as he studied me.

"Hey," I replied in a flat tone.

"Look, everyone is doing the best they can to ensure you're protected. Sometimes our methods suck, but believe me when I tell you that there are times when ignorance is bliss."

When I simply blinked at him without responding, he ran a hand through his hair, leaving it standing up haphazardly. I hated to admit it was a sexy look for him.

My steam was fading, and my shoulders slumped. "I get it, Alessio, but you can't keep me in the dark forever. I'm not stupid—"

"I never said you were," he interrupted, but I held up a hand.

"Let me finish."

He nodded.

"I'm fully aware of who your family is. I also understand that what my father used to do was probably much more dangerous than he led my mom and me to believe. But there is something here"—I waved my hand between him and me—"and it's not just sex. Unless I *am* an idiot and those feelings are totally one-sided. With who your family is, I would think you would want to keep me in the loop to keep me prepared. It would make more sense to ensure I'm vigilant and aware so I don't get bombarded or someone doesn't get a jump on me. Right?"

He dropped his head a second and he wet his lower lip.

Then he met my gaze full-on. "I understand. And there are some things I need to tell you, but this isn't the time."

"Then when is the right time?" I demanded.

"Just give me—" He didn't finish because my iPad dinged. I frowned as I glanced at it in confusion, forgetting I'd signed into the WiFi so I could check my emails.

My iMessages had popped up with a notification.

Unknown Caller: Ask your little boyfriend why he was supposed to kill you

Disbelief lodged my words in my throat. At first, all I could get out was a whimper.

My chest tightened painfully, and I choked out, "You were going to kill me?"

"Fuck," he whispered, and I dragged my attention from my screen to look at him.

Those electric blue eyes practically burned through me before he flattened his lips and closed them. "Yes. But that was be—"

"Don't," I gasped as I held up a hand, the other clutching my tablet to my body.

Rapidly, I blinked, trying my best to dispel the tears before they fell. My lungs were frozen, unable to bring much needed oxygen to my body. Before I could collapse and break down in front of him, I turned and rushed for the bathroom.

Only after I was in the safety of the small room did I crumble. Leaning against the door, I slid down until I was sitting. In a desperate attempt to breathe, I sucked in shallow inhales until I exhaled on a sob.

"Niv, please let me explain," I heard him say through the door.

"Go away. I don't want to talk to you," I called out in a voice watery from crying. I heard a small sound, then the door shook slightly. I could practically picture him with his head resting on the door.

He must've decided to grant my request because I heard him leave and the bedroom door closed.

Then I blinked down at the message that taunted me and started a new message to my dad.

Me: Come get me out of here. Now. Please

Dad: Be there in a sec

I didn't ask him how he knew exactly where I was, and he didn't ask me why. I assumed Alessio made up some story about me pouting in the bathroom or something. Hell, maybe he told him the truth.

Me: Hurry

Dad: I'm here, sweetheart

The knock on the door was followed by my dad's voice through the door. "Honey, I'm here."

I got to my feet and opened the door a crack. "You're alone?" I asked, hating the way my voice cracked.

"Yeah."

I swung it wide and pushed past. After stuffing my iPad and the few things I had left sitting out into the bag, I put it over my shoulder. "Let's go. I want to go see Mom for a while."

He nodded and we walked out together. I had a deadline on my sculpture, but I would email them and tell them

I needed a little more time due to the death of my biological father. They would understand.

As we hit the common area, Alessio stood up from the table with Facet and few others.

"Nivea," he started, but I ducked my head and hurried past, thankful my dad stayed with me.

"Nivea!" Alessio shouted. In my periphery I saw him lunge for me, but chairs scraped and the men he'd been sitting with held him back.

I rushed out the door and fell against the side of the building. My chest caved and I couldn't breathe. Tears burned my eyes and my throat. My brain was scrambled and all I could think was he was supposed to kill me.

Alessio was supposed to kill me.

Dad burst out of the building, and he helped me into his truck. Once we were on the road, he glanced my way. "You wanna tell me what that was about?"

"I got a message from Jade," I whispered.

"What?" My dad's head whipped to stare at me with wide eyes before returning to the road.

"Yeah, I know. She told me to 'ask my boyfriend why he was supposed to kill me.' The whole time, he was the enemy. She hired *him* to kill me. Was this a sick joke to him?" My tears broke through the dam and flowed down my cheeks.

"Nivea. There's no way she messaged you."

"I have the message on my iPad," I assured him.

"No, Niv. She couldn't have messaged you—she's dead."

"How do you know that?" I shot a startled look at him.

"Because I killed her," he grimly replied.

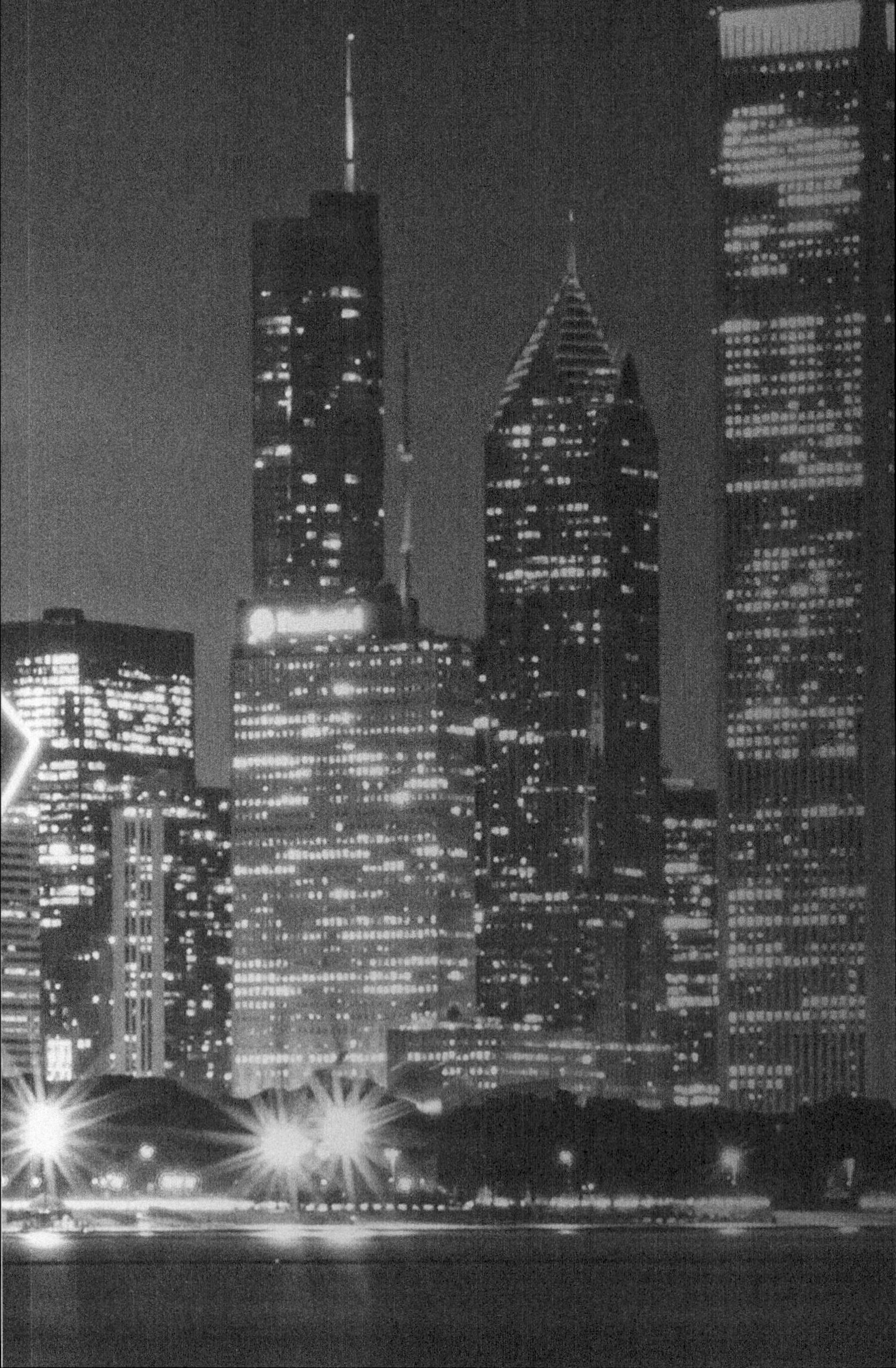

Chapter Ten

Alessio

"WHAT WOULD YOU DO?"—SEETHER

I knew I fucked up, but I didn't expect her to run. When I'd jumped up to get to her, Facet, Sabre, Voodoo, and Chains had seen the look Matt shot me and jumped up. They all stepped in front of me and two of them held me back. I fought them, but they held firm.

"Nivea!" I shouted, but she rushed out the door.

Matt paused at the door to shoot a glare at me. If looks alone could kill, I'd have dropped dead. Then he shook his head. "I told you so. You had a week to tell her and you didn't."

"Don't take her from me!" I broke down and begged.

He coldly stared at me. Then he stormed out after his daughter. It wasn't until I heard his truck start up and pull away that Facet and the boys let me go.

"Do you have a death wish?" Facet snarled in my face.

"She thinks I wanted to kill her!" I growled back.

"You were hired to kill her. Why didn't you tell her if he made it clear you needed to?" Facet's chin lifted as he waited for my reply.

"It wasn't foremost in my mind. There is someone out there who is coming after her and likely me. I had other priorities!" I argued. My heart was slamming into my ribs and my hands shook. I clenched them into fists in an attempt to stop it.

She had left, and not on the best terms. I was convinced she was never going to speak to me again. It was crazy to acknowledge that I was head over heels for a chick over the period of less than a month, but there was no denying it. I'd known she was different right away, but I just hadn't known to what extent.

In my line of work, relationships were a liability. One I wasn't willing to risk. Because of that, I'd never allowed myself to get emotionally entangled with anyone. Except she had snuck past my defenses without me knowing and now it was too late.

"Give her some time. She's with Matt, so you know she's safe. While she has time to settle, we figure out who's after the two of you. If we can stop them, then you should be in the clear. Matt already took out the stepmom, so she's not going to hire anyone else," he explained, and my shoulders drooped as my fury deflated.

"Wait. How the hell did she find out?" My spine straightened as I turned to stare Facet in the eye. "It doesn't make sense."

"I don't have the faintest idea," Facet murmured with his brows drawn together. He looked to Voodoo, who gave him a chin lift.

"Let me see what I can find out," Voodoo murmured before he left.

"You think he can actually find that out?" I asked skeptically.

"If anyone can, it's him," Facet explained. "While he's doing that, let's see if we can track down the other hit man. Then we can make a plan for how you can get her to talk to your dumb ass."

"Fine," I grumbled.

"I'll let you know the minute I find anything out. You'd be wise to stay here, but you're a grown ass man and I'm not gonna tell you what to do." Facet walked off and down the hall that led to his room where he kept his high-tech shit.

I pulled out my phone and called my brother.

"Where the fuck are you?" Vittorio ground out.

"With Facet," I told him. "Why?"

"Because the widow of one Justin Santino is dead after falling down the stairs. Word on the street is that there is a biological daughter that had surfaced about a year ago and is now MIA. The cops are trying to find her because they have some questions for her," he explained.

"Shit," I muttered. "Luciano tell you that?"

"Maybe."

"I'll call her father," I told him as I pinched the bridge of my nose.

"Explain."

In the briefest way I could, I told him everything that had happened since we left.

"Jesus Christ. What a fucking mess. Is there anything we can do?"

"No. But if that changes, I'll let you know. Tell Gabriel where I am and that I'll be in touch when I can." We ended the call, and I went to find Facet.

I knocked on his door and at first there wasn't an answer. Confused, I wondered if he had gone somewhere else. When I was about to walk off, I heard him call out to come in.

The minute I opened the door, the scent of incense filled my nose and there was a strange heaviness in the dark space. It quickly dissipated and I figured I must've imagined it.

"Anything yet?" I asked, then stopped short. "Facet? You okay?"

My friend stood in the center of the room, and I could've sworn his eyes were glowing silver. They dimmed and the flames on the candles sitting on several surfaces flared brighter, then went back to normal.

He blinked a few times, then walked to his desk and sat down. My confused gaze watched him as his fingers flew over the keyboard. "Facet?"

"Yeah?" he asked me, as if he hadn't realized I was in the room.

"I asked if you were okay."

He gave me a questioning tilt of his head and a half smile. "Of course I am, why?"

"I… nothing," I replied. "Anything I can help with?"

"No but pull up a chair." He motioned to a second rolling desk chair, and I grabbed it and sat next to him. For about an hour, he quietly worked, occasionally asking me random questions.

He still hadn't heard anything when Voodoo stuck his head in the door. "I have news."

"Whatcha got?" Facet asked, leaning back and roughing his hair up with his hand.

He set his phone down next to us. "You still there Granmé?"

"I'm here, my boy," I heard a woman say through the speaker.

"Can you tell Facet and our friend Alessio what you saw?" Voodoo asked her.

"Your girl got a message."

"A message? How?" I asked. "She hasn't had her phone since the day we were shot at."

"I saw her with a small tablet. There was very clearly a message on there that upset her."

I thought back to when I walked in the room and she pulled a small iPad to her chest. Fuck. It hadn't registered at the time. I hadn't had a clue she had it with her or that she had access to WiFi.

"Do you know who it was from?" I asked, my mind trying to think of who it could've been. Maybe the guy that was after us had sent it, trying to get her to panic and leave, putting her out in the open. If that was the case, he knew she was here and likely knew she had indeed left.

"I don't. Whoever it was is surrounded by a very dark aura that is blocking me from seeing through." Her tone was ominous and that made a chill skate down my spine.

Then my attention darted to the phone. "Can you tell *where* he is?"

"Let me try."

There was a bunch of rustling and some clinking sounds. It sounded like she dropped a bunch of items. Then she was quiet for so long I had to look at the screen to see if the call was still connected.

Finally, she sighed. "It looked like maybe Chicago?"

A mix of relief that he hadn't known where we were and that he wasn't near where Nivea was. There was no way her dad took her to Chicago. He would've taken her home, if anywhere.

"Thanks, Granmé," Voodoo said with a fond smile.

"Anytime, my boy, anytime. Now when are you bringing my great-grandson down to see me?" She briskly asked him. He chuckled and gave us a wave before he left the room with his phone.

I knew from my research that Nivea's parents lived in California. Her mom was an heiress to a tech empire with more money that even Justin Santino. Her dad, Matt, had been very good at burying his past and his secret side because I hadn't come across a peep of it. I now regretted that I hadn't had Facet look into them instead. In the beginning, he'd offered to look into Nivea, but I had told him I could do that part.

"Wanna help me flush out a killer?" I asked Facet before pressing my lips flat.

"You wanna be bait?" His eyes narrowed.

"Might as well," I replied with a lift of one shoulder.

"Let me talk to Venom and Chains," Facet murmured as he stood up and left the room.

I dropped my elbows to my thighs and buried my face in my hands. What I had in mind could be dangerous, but if I couldn't take care of shit so there were no worries about Nivea's safety, then there was no point. Because the last thing I wanted was to worry about Nivea's safety if she insisted on returning to Chicago.

Because if I knew her, the moment she learned Jade was dead, she'd want to go home. I could only hope her dad could get her to see reason. Because he, as well as anyone in our line of work, knew the ball was already rolling. Whoever else Jade had hired wasn't going to stop until its target was obliterated.

So I was going to flush them out.

Facet returned with Chains and Squirrel. Chains leaned against the wall and crossed his ink covered arms. The ever-present thin leather gloves covered his hands.

Squirrel dropped into the recliner in the corner and observed.

"So what's the plan?" Chains asked.

I grinned, and we began to plot.

Then we left for Chicago.

I'd made myself known once I got back to Chicago. I stopped by my brother's office, I went out to the club owned by The Family, and I ate out at multiple restaurants. Each time, I ensured no one could get a clear shot at me.

I also called Matt every day to check on Nivea and to see if he would let me talk to her.

"I don't like this," Gabriel muttered as we sat in the club's VIP area with his girl, Alia. Vittorio and Kendall would be there soon.

"I have things under control," I assured him.

"But do you?" my oldest brother, the don, grumbled. He was a control freak and hated that this was so unpredictable.

Then, after the night at the club, I made sure it was obvious I was going for a trip and drove in my convertible to my brother's lake home.

We decided to draw him in there. It was more secluded than risking a bunch of civilian casualties since he'd already shown he didn't give a shit about being obvious.

Once I was there, I went inside.

My brows shot up in surprise when I found Angel with the rest of the boys. "I wasn't expecting you."

"Yeah, well, when Voodoo told me you were putting yourself out there all week for someone to use as target practice, I thought you might need me," Angel explained with a smirk. Then he stood, and I walked to him. I gripped his hand and gave his arm a squeeze with my free one.

"Are you ready for this?" Facet asked me from the dining room where he had several laptops spread out on the table. One of them was hooked up to a large monitor and had all of the camera footage on it. He and his boys had come up here early to prepare.

"As I can be." I had slipped into my zone. It had taken a lot, but I was able to put Nivea in a safe place in my mind. My emotions were locked down tight, and I was sharp. "Looks like you have everything set?"

"Yeah. It helps that Gabriel has some high-tech security here. He must've had a serious badass install it," Facet replied with a smirk. He had installed the majority of it and updated a lot that was already here. The property was surrounded by eight-foot wrought iron fencing that had sensors that would set off a silent alarm if anyone touched it. The cameras would lock onto whichever zone was tripped and we'd see if it was an animal or human.

God help them if it was a human.

The hunter had become the hunted and I didn't like that shit one bit. I sure as hell wasn't going to sit around and hide.

"And now we wait," Squirrel chimed in as he gave me a confident grin. "The motherfucker won't know what hit him."

It took four and a half days.

Finally, as I was sitting out on the patio, overlooking the lake, with the umbrella blocking my head from the only open direction for a good shot. I was counting on him taking a shot at my right shoulder or arm in the hopes that would fall and he'd have a head or heart shot.

As I lifted my coffee to my lips, there was a zip sound and my cup fell from my hand as blood splattered on the table from my arm.

"Fuck!" I gritted, fighting my instinct to drop the umbrella as a visual shield like I had at the restaurant that day. He needed to think he'd wounded me enough that he could move in and finish the job. My arm hurt like a bitch and I held my hand over the wound. Red seeped between my fingers and my head swam as a chill shook me.

Agony ripped through me as another bullet pierced through my back and exited my chest. I couldn't breathe. Each sound was wet and gasping.

Glancing down, I saw I was losing a lot of blood.

Still, I held my ground.

The seconds ticked by. Right as black started to creep into the edges of my vision, Angel rushed up to me, cutting my shirt off to expose the bullet holes. Squirrel seemed to just… appear next to the table, making me think I was losing my mind.

"You… got… him?" I choked out when I saw the crimson staining Squirrel's hand and arm.

He nodded and relief hit me. Then the black closed in and I face planted on the table.

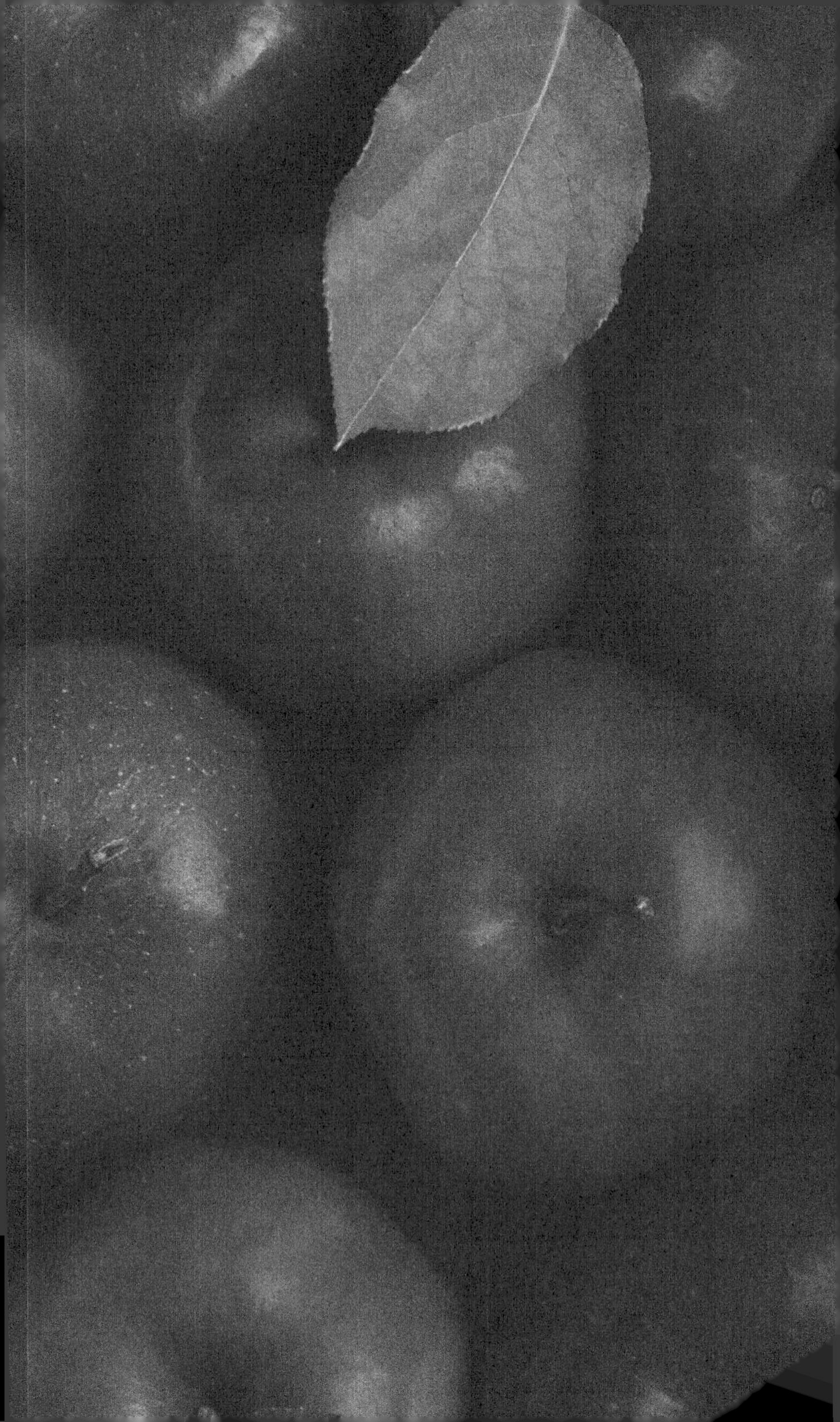

Chapter Eleven

Nivea

"SUMMERTIME SADNESS"—LANA DEL REY

"Niv?" My mom peeked her head in my childhood room, and I listlessly lifted my gaze to her face. The worry in her golden eyes made me feel guilty for moping. I just couldn't help it. My heart was ripped apart and I was bleeding out on the inside.

"Your dad wanted to talk to you," she said when I didn't speak.

A sigh slipped from my lips, and I slowly sat up.

I didn't bother trying to smooth my hair or straighten my clothes. Instead, I got to my feet and shuffled behind my mom as we went to my dad's office. When Mom held the door open, I went in. As I passed, she ran a loving hand from my crown, down the back of my head, to my back before her hand fell away.

Dad sat behind his massive desk, seeming larger than life.

"Yeah?" I asked without emotion as I stopped in front of him.

"Facet called me."

Facet? Not Alessio?

At the thought of his name, my heart flutters then takes off. I hate that he has the power to affect me this way. I hate that I gave him that power by letting him fool me. It's not fair.

My father pauses and a look of pain briefly passes over his features. With that look, I knew, but I had to know for sure.

"Alessio?" I whispered.

"He was shot."

The softly spoken words pull a keening wail from my throat and I drop to my knees. My chest caves and a burning follows. My dad is kneeling next to me, cupping my face as my throat aches and tears pour over his fingers.

"Is he?" I couldn't say the word.

"Facet said he should be okay, but he almost didn't make it."

Relief rips a cry from me as I tremble.

"You really did fall for him, didn't you?" His words are sad, and his thumb brushes away my tears that just keep flowing.

"I only knew him about a month. How did that happen? It doesn't make sense. He was supposed to kill me," I sobbed. "He's a killer, Dad."

I didn't realize my mom had come back until she was kneeling on the other side of me with her arms wrapped around me. Her forehead rested against my temple.

"It doesn't always make sense, baby. Did we ever tell you how we really met—your dad and I?" Mom asked.

"You met in the grocery store parking lot. Right?" I sniffled. "When you ran your cart into Dad's car."

Mom took a deep breath and let it out. "Not exactly."

I blinked my tears away as I frowned in confusion. My head tilted and I gave her a questioning look.

"I had been kidnapped by several of my father's former business associates. They had hired a man to abduct me, and they were holding me for ransom. Your grandfather gave up on law enforcement finding me. I had given up on making it home alive. Then my captor became my extractor." Her golden gaze implored me to understand what she wasn't saying.

"Wait... what?"

"I kidnapped her," my father reluctantly admitted.

My astonished gaze darts to my dad as my butt drops to my heels. "You *stole* Mom?"

Dad winced and lifted one shoulder. Then his gaze hardened. "Nivea, it was a job. But once I got to know your mom... I couldn't follow through with the job I'd been hired to do."

What the actual fuck? "Are you telling me they were never going to actually give her back? That you were supposed to kill her? But grandpa loved you," I sputtered.

"He never knew the truth," my dad admitted. I was shell-shocked.

"The *only* reason I'm telling you this is because, from what your dad told me, Alessio saved you and did his best to keep you safe. He has called for you every day," Mom murmured.

My attention flew to my father as I gaped at him and my mom in disbelief. "Why didn't you tell me?"

"Because he was an asshole for not telling you the truth when I told him he needed to," my father grumbled.

"I told you she should know," Mom snapped.

"Am I the only one who is remembering that he was going to kill our daughter?" Dad practically shouted.

"But he ended up saving her instead," my mom quietly replied as she laid her palm gently to my dad's cheek.

My dad's jaw clenched. Then resignation filled his gaze.

"He was able to stop the other hitman Jade hired," he finally admitted.

My brain was scrambled. My reality was skewed. I had a hard time processing everything. History had essentially been repeating itself. What a mindfuck. It left me feeling… numb.

"So I can go home?"

"If you want. Though I wish you'd stay here," Dad replied.

"I want."

Dad sighed. "I'll call to have the plane prepared."

"Thank you," I whispered.

Despite my initial devastation when I thought Alessio was gone, and the truth I'd learned about my parents, I wasn't sure things would ever work out between him and me. We weren't my parents. My heart would never be the same, but he lived in such a different world than I did.

Who cares? The connection you had was like fate created it.

That little voice prodded at me. I ignored it.

Then I got up and gathered my things to go home.

I'd been home a week. My sculpture was finally finished and shipped off to Texas.

Alessio had been calling my business phone after I'd shut my personal phone off after the first day. My business one was a necessity. And he damn well knew it.

God, I wanted to answer those calls.

I wanted to hear his voice.

Hell, I dreamed about him.

My hands smoothed slowly over the warm clay, shaping and molding. I picked up the tool I wanted and used it to carve the details the way I saw them in my mind. When I was done, I tilted my head to study my work.

A sad smile lifted one side of my mouth.

Because looking back at me was the face of the man that wouldn't leave my head. I ran a clay-stained finger down the slope of his nose. Then I fell back in my chair in disgust.

My gaze flickered over to the other two I'd already made. The first one had a fist shaped dent in the middle of its handsome face.

Should I call him back?

Could we ever work?

My phone dinged. With a heavy heart, I stood up and

went to the sink to wash my hands. As I was drying them, there was a knock on my door. I frowned.

An itty-bitty glimmer of hope hit my heart and spread warmth through me. Despite my stubbornness, I prayed it might be him. If it was, I was going to cave. Having him in front of me would be too hard to resist. I had been thinking a lot and over the past week, and I realized I'd forgiven him.

Maybe it made me a nutcase, but it was true.

Then I wove around my furniture to the door, my steps lighter. However, a glance through the peephole left me bewildered. I opened it.

"Carl?" I asked with a tilt of my head.

He gave me a sad smile. "Hi, Nivea. Can I come in?"

"Of course," I stepped back and urged him in. "What brings you over?"

"I wanted to check on you. I feel bad that I hadn't done so since Justin's passing. Things just got so…." He gave me a helpless lift of his hands.

"Crazy?" I supplied, and he gave a humorless laugh.

"You could say that." The poor man looked so sad. I knew he had been with Justin for quite a while. His death must have been devastating for him. Then for Jade to go so soon after—even though I sure as hell didn't mourn the bitch—she had also been his boss, I supposed.

"Do you want something to drink?" I asked him as I headed back to the kitchen.

"Oh, no thank you. I just brought you something that I thought you deserved," he murmured.

I was touched that he might've come across something

of Justin's that he thought I would want. "Aw, thank you," I softly said as I turned around to face him.

He nodded as he reached into his pocket.

Except what he brought out wasn't a gift.

He was firmly holding a revolver with the muzzle pointed directly at my chest.

"Carl?" I whispered in surprise and fear.

The previously timid and soft-spoken man was suddenly cold, with a hard glint in his muddy colored eyes. "You couldn't be happy with what you had, could you?"

"What?"

"You had a family, money, and a successful career. You didn't need Justin. Still, you crawled out of the woodwork and ruined *everything*."

My mouth fell open. For a moment, I was speechless.

"I couldn't believe it when he changed his will to leave most of his fortune to you. I had a plan and you fucked it all up," he sneered and I was taken aback. This was not the man I'd known.

"You killed Justin," I murmured as some of the pieces fell into place. "So you're going to just shoot me? For what?" I glanced around for my phone. If I could find it, I could hit the SOS feature my dad had set up. But I needed to distract Carl and buy some time.

"Oh, I'm not going to shoot you," he replied with a calculating stare.

"You're not?" I asked, confused.

"No. You were so distraught at the death of your biological father followed so quickly by your stepmother's death that you killed yourself." He gave me a smile, like what he said made complete and total sense.

"But I would never do that," I argued, looking at him like he was insane, which I was pretty sure he was.

"Once you're gone, no one would know that, would they? People hide mental illnesses all the time. Now get moving. Open that window." He motioned at me with the gun and pointed to one of my industrial windows with it.

"Carl," I tried, thinking I might be able to reason with him. "I won't accept any of the money. Or if I do, I'll turn it over to you," I lied.

"You think I believe you? You ruined everything! You think I don't know you had something to do with Jade's death? You're a lying, greedy little bitch," he snarled, his expression rapidly morphing.

My chin jerked back in disbelief at the instant change in his personality.

"You… you… you thought you were going to be with Jade and you two would live happily ever after with Justin's money?" I stammered. He was unbelievable. My eyes snagged on my phone at the end of my kitchen counter.

His head fell back as a maniacal laugh erupted from the squat little man. I moved closer to my phone but froze when his attention returned to me.

"With Jade? Are you delusional? That heartless bitch wouldn't have stayed with me long after she had Justin's money. She thought she was manipulating me into killing Justin, but she wasn't nearly as smart as she thought she was. I planned to get her to marry me by threatening to go to the police with what we'd done, then I was going to kill her—and everything would go to me. Except you took care of her before I could get everything done." By the time he finished his tirade, he was spitting with his words. Saliva gathered at the corners of his mouth.

"Carl, that never would've worked," I tried to rationalize in hopes that I could get him to keep talking. I took another tiny step toward my phone.

"It would have! But you fucked it up. If I can't have what I want, neither can you. Now get moving!" He cocked the hammer back and I swallowed hard.

Heart slamming in my chest, I beat myself up. I hated that I'd ignored Alessio's attempts to contact me. Now he'd never know how I felt.

Slowly, I walked to the window and opened it. When I paused, he held the gun to my temple. My breath hitched. It was in that moment that my regret hit me like a tsunami. If only I had replied to Alessio's text messages or answered his calls. I should've talked to him. Because regardless of what he'd been hired to do, he didn't—instead, he saved me.

And he made me feel more beautiful than I'd ever felt in my life.

But he'd never know… because I'd been so damn stubborn.

"Y-Y-You won't shoot me. Y-Y-You want it to look like a suicide," I stuttered.

"And I can do that with the gun just as easily. I just didn't want your brain matter all over my new shoes," he sneered. "Now get up there."

"Carl! Please!" I cried.

Hands shaking, I gripped the frame and lifted my foot up to the sill. Everything I wish I could do ran through my head. But it was too late.

"Now, Jump!" Carl playfully whispered.

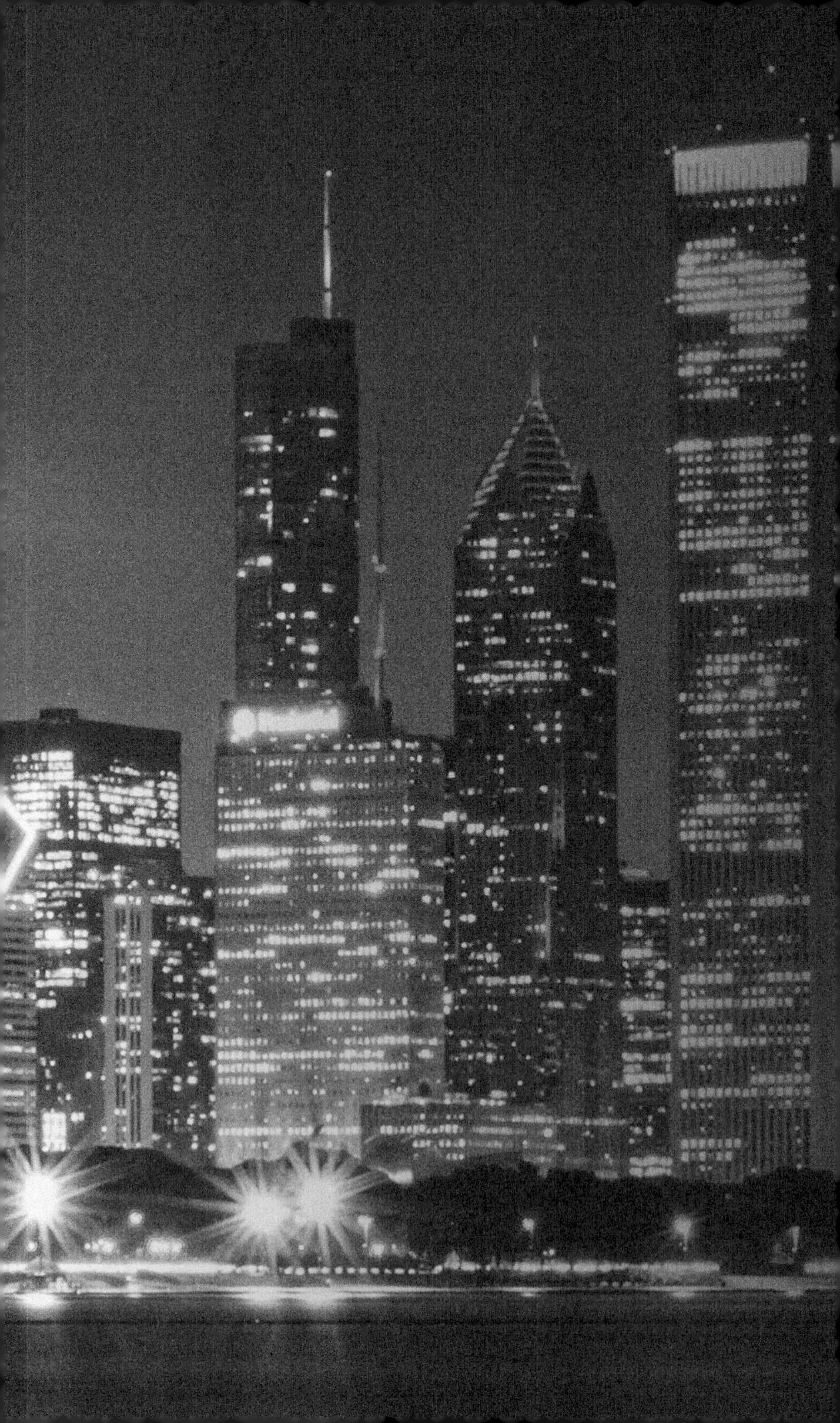

Chapter Twelve

Alessio

"ALL SIGNS POINT TO LAUDERDALE"—A DAY TO REMEMBER

> Me: I've had enough. I'm coming over whether you like it or not. We need to talk

I sent the text and climbed into the back of the black Cadillac XTS sedan. I told my driver where I wanted to go and we pulled out into traffic.

After a couple of brief stops, we made our way to Nivea's condo.

"Do you want me to wait?" my driver asked.

"Just until I know if she's actually here," I absently replied, then went into the building. The ride to the top floor seemed to take forever. When I got out, I marched to her door, prepared to knock it down if I had to. The stubborn woman was going to hear me out.

But when I reached up to knock, I heard voices coming from inside. "Shit," I whispered, hoping it wasn't her father. The man would probably beat my ass before I could say a word to her.

Then I heard her cry out, and I almost dropped the bag of food and flowers, but I would lose the element of surprise. Cautiously, I set them to the side and tried the door. It was locked, so I pulled out my wallet. I slipped the lock pick from it and quickly picked her knob, hoping the deadbolt wasn't locked as well. Those could sometimes be a little tricky.

Relief hit me when I was able to open the door after unlocking the knob. Quietly, I turned it and debating barging in or opening the door slowly to draw less attention. The layout of her condo was pretty open, so I wouldn't have much cover. There was a chance she was arguing with her father, but she had sounded scared, not angry.

What I saw when I carefully stepped inside made my blood run cold. In a move born out of muscle memory, I had my pistol in my hand.

The little weasel that was Justin Santino's assistant was holding a gun pointed at Nivea as she stood in her open window, clutching the frame. Her eyes were wide and terrified.

As I raised my weapon, he pushed her and as her feet slipped from the sill, I pulled the trigger. The piece of shit hadn't even hit the floor before I was in motion. Heart in my throat, I prepared myself for the devastation.

What I wasn't expecting was to see the woman I was in love with hanging on for dear life to what looked like a plant ledge.

"Alessio!" She stared up at me with terror in her gaze.

"Fuck. I'm coming," I told her as I leaned over the metal shelf, for lack of better words, to reach for her. But my weight leaning over added with hers caused the metal to creak and it appears to be pulling from the aged brick of the building.

She screamed and I swore. Fighting to stay calm, I glanced around her condo, looking for something I could use to harness her. There had to be something because I didn't know how long she could hold on.

Then I spotted her welder sitting near her work area. She had a long, thick extension cord plugging it in to the wall. Stepping over the dead body, I rushed over, jerked it from the wall, and unplugged it from the machine.

"Niv, baby, I'm going to try to loop this around you so we can use it as a harness to get you up. Hang on for me," I stared her in the eye as I was making the loops—one for her, and one for me. If she fell, I would do my damnedest to be her anchor.

"O-O-Okay," she stuttered.

Christ, her teeth were chattering. It was both freezing out there, and she was likely going into shock. I worked faster, then I wrapped one end around myself and leaned out as far as I could without putting too much weight on the plant shelf.

I tried to use it a bit like a lasso to get it around her lower body, but a cowboy, I sure as fuck was not. Her knuckles were white, but her cheeks and hands were bright red. After two more attempts, I wanted to roar out my frustration and fear.

Taking a deep breath, I tried again. I almost cried when I got it around one foot but not the other. "Baby, I need you to see if you can get your other foot through the loop."

She glanced down and her face went ashen. A whimper carried on the cold wind.

"Try," I encouraged her. "I know you can do this."

She nodded slightly, but I could tell she was trying to convince herself as much as me. She dropped her gaze and tried to slip her other foot through, but the movement only made her start to sway. Her attention snapped back to me. "I can't."

"Yes. You. Can. Do you hear me? You can do this." I stared into her terrified blue eyes and prayed to a god I really didn't believe in anymore to help her.

"Y-Y-Yes." She tried again and almost had it. Then a determined look hit her face and she did it again. That time it connected, and the loop was around her lower legs.

"When I get it up to your chest, I need you to grab it with one hand. When I tell you, you let go of the railing with the other and I'll pull you up."

Her lower lip trembled, but she nodded.

Carefully, I worked the loop up. I didn't want to do it too quickly and have it just slip off. When it was where I hoped would be the best area, I locked my gaze on her with more confidence than I really felt. "You ready?"

"No," she quietly replied.

I breathed heavily out of my nose. "You're going to be okay," I promised her.

She let go with one hand and grabbed the thick cord. I braced my feet and legs against the wall better. "Ready? Now grab on with the other hand and keep the loop in your armpits, okay?"

"Okay," she whispered.

This was probably going to leave some hellacious bruises

on us both, but better that than the alternative. "Come on, baby. When you start to come over the ledge, you're gonna need to use your legs to help pull yourself over so I don't hurt you by just dragging you over."

Slowly, I watched as her fingers peeled away from the rail. Her weight hit me, and I gritted my teeth as I fought to hold her and pull her up. Leaning back, I stepped away from the window, trying to avoid the pool of blood that had seeped around the body. At what seemed like a snail's pace, I dragged her up.

The metal screws groaned and creaked. As her torso cleared the window frame, there was a horrific sound and one side broke free. Nivea screamed and I hoped no one heard her or saw what was happening and called the cops.

"It's fine. You don't need it. Try to push up with your legs against the building," I encouraged.

Determination pinched her face and my pride in her exploded.

After what seemed an eternity, she scrambled through the window and collapsed to the floor.

I immediately scooped her up with trembling arms and buried her face against my shoulder. I didn't want her looking at Justin's assistant laying lifeless on the floor. I stumbled backward and dropped my ass to the chair in her living room area. The entire time, I held onto her for dear life.

"You saved me," she breathed the words against my neck. "Again."

"Baby, I'm not good enough for you, but I will always save you."

She clung to me as our heartbeats began to slow and our breaths calmed. I didn't let her go either.

"I'm sorry I didn't tell you the truth right away. The minute I realized you were the most kind-hearted person I'd ever met, I knew there was no way you did what your stepmother said you did. I should've told you then." I kissed her temple.

"I'm sorry I ran off," she murmured into my neck.

"I understand."

We sat there and held each other in silence for a while. My cheek rested on her head. I knew I needed to make a call to Facet to have them come in and clean up this mess, but I didn't want to let her go.

"D-D-Did you kill him?" she stuttered.

I wasn't going to lie to her. That hadn't served us well in the past. "Yes. And I'd do it again. I'd slay someone with my bare hands if they were trying to hurt you. I'm not a good man, and I sure as hell don't deserve you. But you mean everything to me—I love you. Crazy as it might sound to some, considering the short period of time I've known you, I do."

A sob shook her frame. "I love you too. And I don't care if people say were being impulsive, crazy, or dumb. I know what I feel."

I stood with her in my arms, wincing at the pain where the electrical cord had practically cut into me. She sucked in a sharp breath and I knew I needed to check her over too.

Making my way through her open condo, I found her room and brought her to her bed. Gently, I set her down. "I need to make sure you're okay," I explained.

She nodded and I removed her hoodie and T-shirt. She

wasn't wearing a bra and I had to squeeze my eyes shut a moment. I willed my dick to behave. After all, we'd both nearly lost each other—this wasn't the time. The bruising was already forming on her body, and I cringed. I settled her in the bed and crawled on top of the covers to hold her.

It didn't take long before she was asleep. The trauma sapped every bit of energy she had.

Trying not to wake her, I dug my phone out of my pocket. I shot off a text to Facet, who was still at my condo with the boys. Next, I messaged her father. Finally, I laid my head down next to her and dozed off.

By the time Facet and the boys arrived, I had gotten up without waking Niv and went out to the living room, where they waited.

Angel was crouched by Justin's assistant. I think his name was Carl.

"There's nothing I can do," Angel said.

"Good," I muttered.

Angel assessed my damage and frowned. "Are you *trying* to undo all my work?"

I shook my head. "I'm fine."

"It's not that bad. It won't take much out of me. Let me rest up and I'll take care of your girl, too."

"No. Her first."

"Stubborn ass," Angel muttered.

Trying to ignore the ache from where I knew I was probably bruised, I took him into the bedroom where Nivea still slept. He placed his palms on her back and closed his eyes.

It didn't take long, but when he removed them, he stumbled back a step.

"Come on." I hooked his arm around my neck and helped him out to the couch. The movement was excruciating, but I gritted through the pain. He collapsed to the cushions and was out like a light. Squirrel and Facet were already rolling the body up in plastic.

"Venom is sending the Mystery Machine, as Cookie called it. It's gonna cost you, though." Facet smirked.

I gave a huff and rubbed the spots on my sides where the cord left friction burns and bruising was already starting to develop.

"Give me a few minutes and I'll take care of you," Angel mumbled from the couch.

"Thanks man, but I'll be fine," I assured him as I waved off his offer.

Squirrel began the initial cleanup of the mess I left after shooting Carl. I grabbed more trash bags and paper towels. He tossed me a pair of rubber gloves.

"You walk around with these in your pockets?" I asked as I looked down at them, then back to him.

He shrugged. "Hey, you never know what you might come across. Present situation a perfect example. Aren't you glad we decided to stick around a few days?"

Sending him, Facet, and Angel a thankful gaze, I nodded. "Yeah, I actually am. Thank you—again."

"That's what friends are for, right? Hiding dead bodies?" Facet added, as he gave me a cocky grin.

It said something for our intestinal fortitude that we

could sit there and joke about something like that after I'd put a bullet through a man's head. In the past, I would've said I could do that with zero emotion.

This time? It had been personal, and the emotions involved had been rage and love. That was when the true realization hit me. Nivea almost died. Had I not decided enough was enough and headed to her place, she would be gone.

That was a sobering thought.

"I can't believe no one called in the gunshot," Squirrel chimed in.

A huffed laugh left me and I shook my head. "This is Chicago. There are so many gunshots here that people rarely get personally involved. With all the buildings around here, anyone that might've been tempted to call it in probably wasn't sure where it came from. And luckily people kind of mind their own business so it's unlikely anyone saw Nivea hanging from the window. If they did, it's the same as the gunshots—don't get involved."

"Oh, and I was going to put some anti-listening devices in the condo for you, but it looked like someone beat me to it," Facet told me.

"Gee, I'll give you two guesses who that would've been." I cocked a brow and Facet laughed.

"Yeah, I should've figured her dad would've covered that here. But I thought you'd like to know they're already installed, working, and some of the most high-tech ones I've ever seen."

"Not surprised." I smiled and shook my head.

"Oh, and the food and flowers you left in the hall? I brought them in for you."

I glanced over to the counter where he had motioned. He had put the flowers in a water pitcher, which didn't surprise me. "Thanks. I appreciate it."

Once I helped them clean up what we could, I went in to check on Nivea. The guys went to get some food and have a couple of beers. They said they'd be back when the van arrived. She was still out like a light, but Angel had warned me she might sleep through the night. In a way, I hoped she did. The last thing I wanted her to wake up to was any evidence of me killing someone in her home.

At first, panic took hold as she nearly seemed still as death. Then the even rise and fall of her chest made me breathe easier. Knowing she was safe comforted me. As I watched her lay there sleeping, I debated kissing her full, red lips. Instead, I pacified myself by pressing a kiss to my fingers, then placing them on the comforter that covered her.

With a soft sigh, she turned to her side.

Unwilling to disturb the rest she needed in order to finish what Angel had started, I tiptoed out of her room and put her cord back where I found it. Nosy, I wandered around, looking over her studio area. I stopped in my tracks when I saw her current work in progress.

It was me.

Down to the barely visible scar at the end of my right eyebrow.

A chill skated over my skin that was soon followed by warmth. Then I noticed there were two more. One with my signature smirk, the other… Jesus, had she caved my face in with her *fist?*

With a grin, I shook my head. My girl was a savage.

On the walls in between the huge windows were prints of her art sculptures. Everything from images of her work in progress to the completed image in its final location.

When I'd started digging into her, I'd seen she was a talented artist, but seeing these candid images blew me away. My favorite one was of her with a welding hood on as she welded the frame for a sculpture. She looked like such a badass, and even though her face wasn't visible, she looked sexy as fuck.

My phone buzzed in my pocket. When I pulled it out, I saw my oldest brother's name.

"Hello, Big Bossman," I answered.

"Really?" Gabriel drily asked me.

"Well, you are. Right?"

"Yes, I am, but I'm not your boss," he replied, and I could hear the smirk. "I was calling to see if you were still in town and if so, would you want to come over for dinner?"

"I am, but I'll have to take a raincheck. I'm dealing with some things right now."

"Everything okay?" The humor was instantly erased from his tone.

Knowing my call was secure, I explained the situation.

"Jesus fucking Christ," Gabriel muttered when I was done. "As long as you and your girl are okay. I'm assuming she's your girl, anyway."

A grin stretched unbidden across my lips. "We still need to iron out a few things, but I certainly hope so."

"That's a yes. And little brother, I couldn't be happier for you. I truly never thought I'd see the day. Now if we could just get Leo to settle down," Gabriel grumbled the last part.

"Have you talked to him?" I asked, staring out at the darkening sky.

"No. I'm assuming you haven't either?"

"No. He was still in Europe the last time I talked to him. He hasn't answered my calls in weeks. I know his ass is still alive because he paid his half of the utilities about a day ago," I said with a sigh.

"He's getting out of hand. It's time for him to pull his head out of his ass and figure out what he's going to do with his life." Gabriel had been just as worried about Leo as Vittorio and I had been since Francesco died. As his twin, Leo took it the hardest. At first, none of us blamed him for going off the rails. It just hadn't gotten any better, and in my opinion, it was getting worse. I was afraid we would get a call that he was dead somewhere too, but not from an enemy. At least not one that wasn't himself.

"I'm thinking of taking some time off. Maybe I can get him to spend some time with me and Niv," I mused. Someone tried to call me, but I let it go to voicemail.

"Good luck with that. Anyway, I'm sorry about all the shit with your girl. You let me know when things are better for her and we'll arrange a date to have dinner with all of us. We'll invite Leo, but I doubt he'll come," he sighed.

"Yeah, I know. I'll keep in touch."

"Sounds good. Love you, little brother."

"Love you too."

We ended the call and I saw I missed a call from Facet. I called him back. "Sorry, I was on the line with the big man."

"No worries, bro. Just wanted to let you know that the Mystery Machine is on its way to you. We're hopping in the truck and heading to you, too. See you shortly."

They arrived after fighting traffic and got to work. I was surprised to see Venom had ridden along with Ghost.

"Alessio? Do you have a minute?" he asked me.

"Sure," I replied and motioned over to the couch in the area designated as a living room.

"I'll take the stiff out to the van," Squirrel offered as he picked the body wrapped in plastic up and tossed it over his shoulder, then chuckled darkly. "It's not like it'll freak him out."

I blinked and he was gone. Then I blinked slowly several times. "What the fuck?"

Venom smirked. "You get used to it."

Yes, I loved that they trusted me with their secrets, but it still tripped me out at times.

We took a seat, and he cocked his head as he silently studied me for a moment. With his uncanny blue-green, gray-green eyes, it was a bit unnerving, but I'd never admit that to him.

"I heard you might be thinking of retiring," Venom quietly murmured.

My brows shot to my hairline, and I pressed my lips flat before I replied. "Oh yeah? Who said that?"

"A little birdie," he cryptically replied as he shrugged.

I figured it was either Voodoo or his grandmother, the voodoo priestess down in the New Orleans area. They had an uncanny ability to see things, which was why Voodoo had reached out to her when everything went down there with Niv and me. It had to be, because the only people I'd discussed it with were people who didn't have a lot of interaction with the RBMC.

"Maybe. Why are you asking?" I hedged.

"Because maybe I have a job offer for you," he replied with a slight lift of his chin as he tugged on one of his lip piercings with his teeth.

"Doing?"

"Well, as you know, we lost Raptor and Phoenix. I'm betting we're gonna lose Blade to Texas too, but he hasn't really said yet. That leaves me short a few hands. The garbage still needs to be taken out, and we could use someone with your talents. I'm not expecting an answer today, but I wanted to make the offer face-to-face. We won't be able to pay what you're getting now, but it would keep you closer to home and you'd have a team to work with instead of flying solo. So think about it." Venom stood, signifying he was done talking. I followed because while I really liked him and the boys, I was anxious to be alone with Niv.

"At this point, I'm not worried about the level I've been getting. I'll definitely think it over. Thank you for trusting me enough to make the offer." We shook hands and then they got busy. That time, I stayed out of the way. They had a system and I'd only slow them down.

Before I knew it, they were bagging up the last of their things and I walked them to the door.

"Thank you again," I told them as I shook their hands.

"Not a problem. It's a pleasure doing business with you," Ghost replied with a smirk and a waggle of his brows. We all laughed.

Venom paused as he gripped my hand. "Think about my offer. If it's something you're interested in, we can discuss details."

"I appreciate it."

Finally, they were gone and there was no sign of what had happened in the condo earlier. I was bone weary and wanted to hold my girl. Hopefully, she didn't wake up and ring my bell.

Rounding in the condo, I made sure all the windows were locked and the lights were off, then I went into Nivea's bedroom.

Undressing, I climbed in behind her. I was past trying to do the right thing. As far as I was concerned, this was the right thing. We'd work out the details later. Hell, maybe I'd take my brother's advice and retire.

Maybe.

Scooting closer, I reveled in the warm curves that I cuddled into. I breathed in her soft hair. Gently, so I didn't wake her, I pressed a kiss to the slope of her shoulder. For a moment, I wondered who this person was that I'd become.

I'd returned to Chicago and become one of the best in my dark and dangerous field. I hadn't wanted or needed a relationship. Yet now, here I was contemplating turning my life on end for one raven-haired temptress. The thing was?

It didn't bother me one bit.

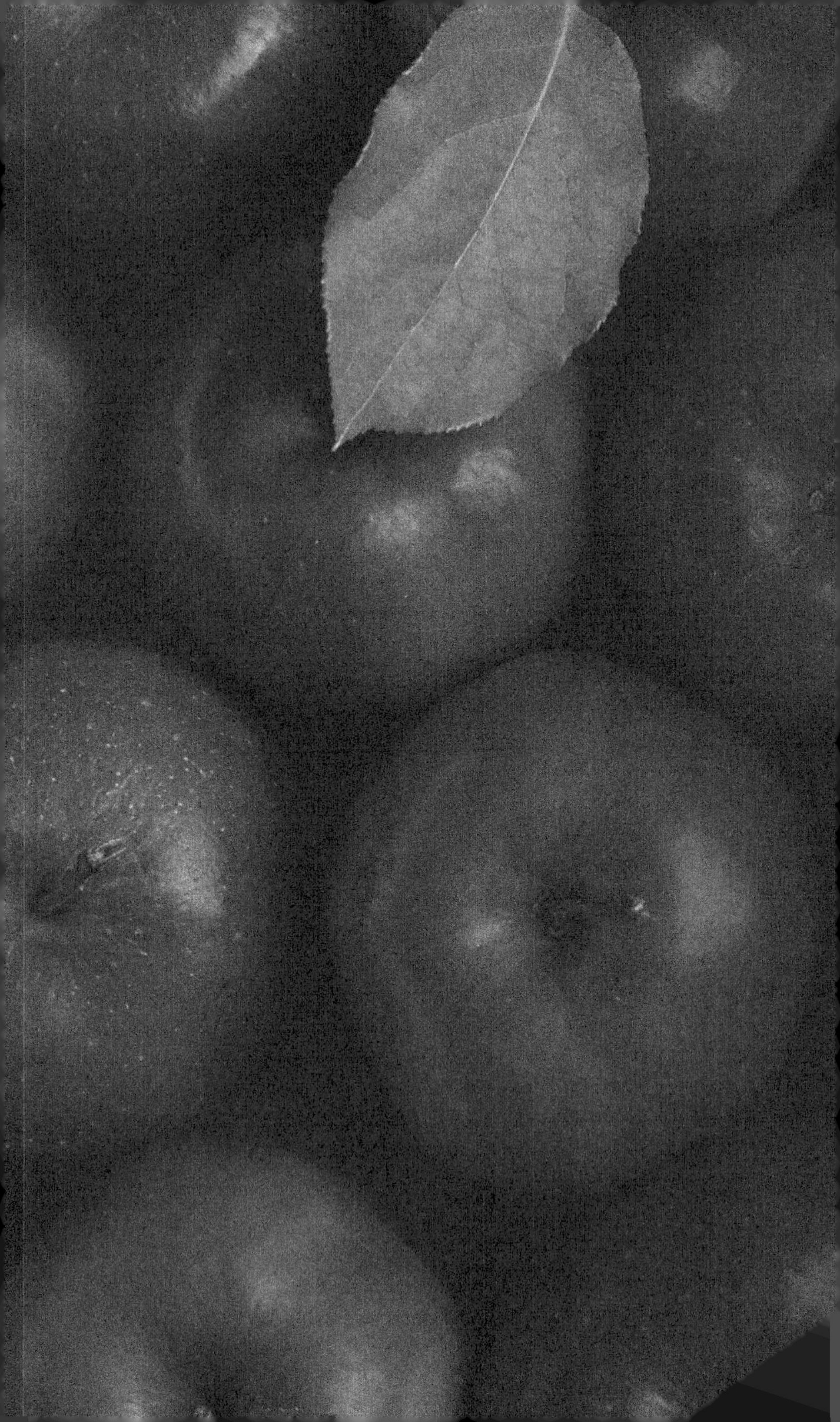

Chapter Thirteen

Nivea

"DANDELIONS"—RUTH B

Two weeks had passed since Carl tried to kill me. Alessio found out that he had been pawning off Justin's lesser valued items and selling some of his more valuable things on the black market. Carl had figured he'd get as much as he could. We also found out he was the one who sent me the message, but we still had no idea why he thought killing me would gain him anything but his hateful revenge.

Though Alessio and I were given a second chance, I was still a little miffed that he hadn't told me he'd been hired to kill me. It ticked me off that he thought I wouldn't have listened to him. Part of the reason I'd been so devastated is because I'd been left feeling like he had lied to me and was toying with me. After I'd had time to think about it, I'd realized he had been nothing but good to me and my overactive imagination had run away with me.

Then again, my emotions were understandably frazzled at that time.

Finished with my welder and set it to the side, then I

flipped up my helmet. With a critical eye, I surveyed my work. A knock on the had me pulling it off.

"I've got it," Alessio called out as he came out of his office. Already, he knew not to come in when I was welding or risk getting flash burn, and to listen for it to be shut off first.

My handsome boyfriend had opened up one of the corner rooms in his condo for me to do my smaller projects on the days I stayed with him. The fact that he hired a crew to come in to do a rush job on a room so it had the appropriate safety measures for me to work had made me cry. He admitted he was prepared to do whatever it took to kiss my ass for not telling me the truth right away.

I might've milked that a bit for the first few days.

The sound of men's voices carried through the massive condo, but I couldn't tell who it was. When Alessio knocked on the doorframe, I glanced over my shoulder at him.

"Everything okay?" I asked because his face looked pale and a little shell-shocked.

"I… uh… there's someone here to see you. But I think you better be prepared for this shit."

I jerked my chin back as I warily stared at him. "Who is it?"

"You should probably just come out," he replied.

Curious, I pulled off my gloves and dropped them on my work bench as I followed him to the living room.

When we got there, a blond man sat on the couch with his back to us. At the sound of our approaching footsteps, he stood up and slowly turned.

My heart stopped and I gasped before my hands flew

over my mouth. Then I dropped them and with a stuttered inhale, I approached the man.

"Justin?" I breathed, barely able to form words. My eyes darted over his features, not believing what I was seeing.

The look of apology and sorrow in his blue eyes hit me straight in the guts.

"I don't understand," I murmured before I threw my arms around him and hugged him tightly. Tears welled, then rolled down my cheeks. He returned my affection with a strong, warm embrace of his own.

Then he proceeded to explain that he had a psychic reading and the medium told him she saw him die—specifically that someone was trying to kill him. He had been consulting this psychic his entire adult life because she had given him valuable advice on numerous occasions, to the point where he credited her for the majority of his fortune he had amassed.

"She also told me about you, but we always assumed you were a future child, not that you were already alive. At least, not until you found me. After that happened, we were both shocked. Then again, she always said she wasn't shown everything, just what I needed to know at the time." He shrugged, but it had me wondering what my life could've been like if we'd known sooner.

Then I decided that if things hadn't happened the way they did, I might have never met Alessio.

Justin ended up working with local Chicago police initially, then the FBI stepped in. They had decided to fake his death after overhearing a suspicious conversation between his wife and his assistant.

"So you caught Carl opening the safe in your home office and helping himself to some of your cash?" I asked, astonished at the little man's audacity.

"I did. He claimed Jade had sent him after it, but that didn't make sense, because Jade would've asked me. Then I heard them arguing about it that night when they didn't realize I had come home early from my business meeting." Justin palmed his face a moment before dropping his arms to the dining room table. "The FBI found out that he'd been pawning my things even back then. What bothered me was that I would've given him money if he needed it. It was simply envy and greed."

"He must've been insane," I gasped.

"I think he was—at least very sociopathic. But sweetheart, I had no idea Carl would go after you. He always seemed to be fond of you."

"I guess he had everyone fooled," Alessio chimed in as he shook his head in disbelief.

"That he did—until he didn't. I ended up telling Jade that my psychic told me I was going to die and it scared me. I led her to believe I decided to prepare for my death on the off-chance. I went and had that paperwork added to my instructions upon death. But I had Carl witness everything at my attorney's office, then told him and Jade that I filed the paperwork and all the information was in the safe as to the funeral home, etc. Jade and Carl then decided it was the perfect time to kill me." The betrayal of the two people he trusted more than anything was visible in the lines that bracketed his mouth and eyes.

"So after what you had heard them saying, you believed they were not only stealing from you but plotting to kill you?" Alessio asked.

Justin nodded. "I had an actual reading after the events that transpired and she really did confirm that someone was trying to kill me—after all that, I believed that it was Carl and Jade. We suspected because of several odd searches Carl had made on my computer. My psychic told me not to eat or drink anything prepared at the house. I told the FBI I had seen and overheard suspicious things that made me fear they were trying to kill me."

"Justin, I'm so sorry. I wish you could've just come to my place and hide out for a while!" I told him.

"After they tried to frame you, it's a good thing I didn't. I guess Carl used the access information you gave me to get into your home. That's why I needed them to believe I had died so the FBI could find the proof they needed and not be a target while they did it. Carl had a PI following me and he told them about the headache herbs you gave me. That coincided with their plan, and that night after we had lunch, Carl poured me a whiskey I hadn't asked for. As instructed, I didn't drink it, but pretended to sip on it until Carl left the room, then poured it down the sink," Justin explained further.

I was flabbergasted. "This is like something out of a book or a movie."

"I'm so sorry you got pulled into it. I had intentionally left everything in trust for an extended period of time so you wouldn't be considered a target. I wasn't counting on Carl's absolute deceitful nature."

"Deceitful? I'd say more like evil," I said with a shudder.

"I just can't believe Jade fell down the stairs before they could get definitive proof on her. Then Carl disappeared. They are wondering if he killed her, then left the country." Justin leaned back in the chair and lifted the cup of coffee I'd made him and took a sip. I imagined it might be cold by that time. He didn't seem to care, but the poor man had been through a shitshow.

Neither Alessio nor I said a word about knowing what really happened to Jade and Carl. It was better that way.

"How did you know where to find me?" I asked Justin, curious now that I thought about the fact that he had no idea Alessio had been hired by Jade to kill me. Therefore, he shouldn't have had any idea to look for me at Alessio's place.

He gave a small, huffed laugh. "My own PI."

We chatted some more, then Justin left with the promise that we would all get together soon—under better circumstances.

"What a clusterfuck," I muttered, still blown away by everything that had transpired—as well as Justin sporting blond hair.

"You can say that again," Alessio agreed. Then he looped his arms around my waist and pulled my flush to his body. I placed my hands flat on his firm chest. "Do you still have a lot of work to do?"

"Not really. Why?"

"Oh, I thought maybe I could do a little more ass-kissing again—literally." His grin was wicked.

And I loved it.

"Oooo, I think that's a brilliant idea." I lifted to my tiptoes and kissed him, then took his hand and led him to his bedroom.

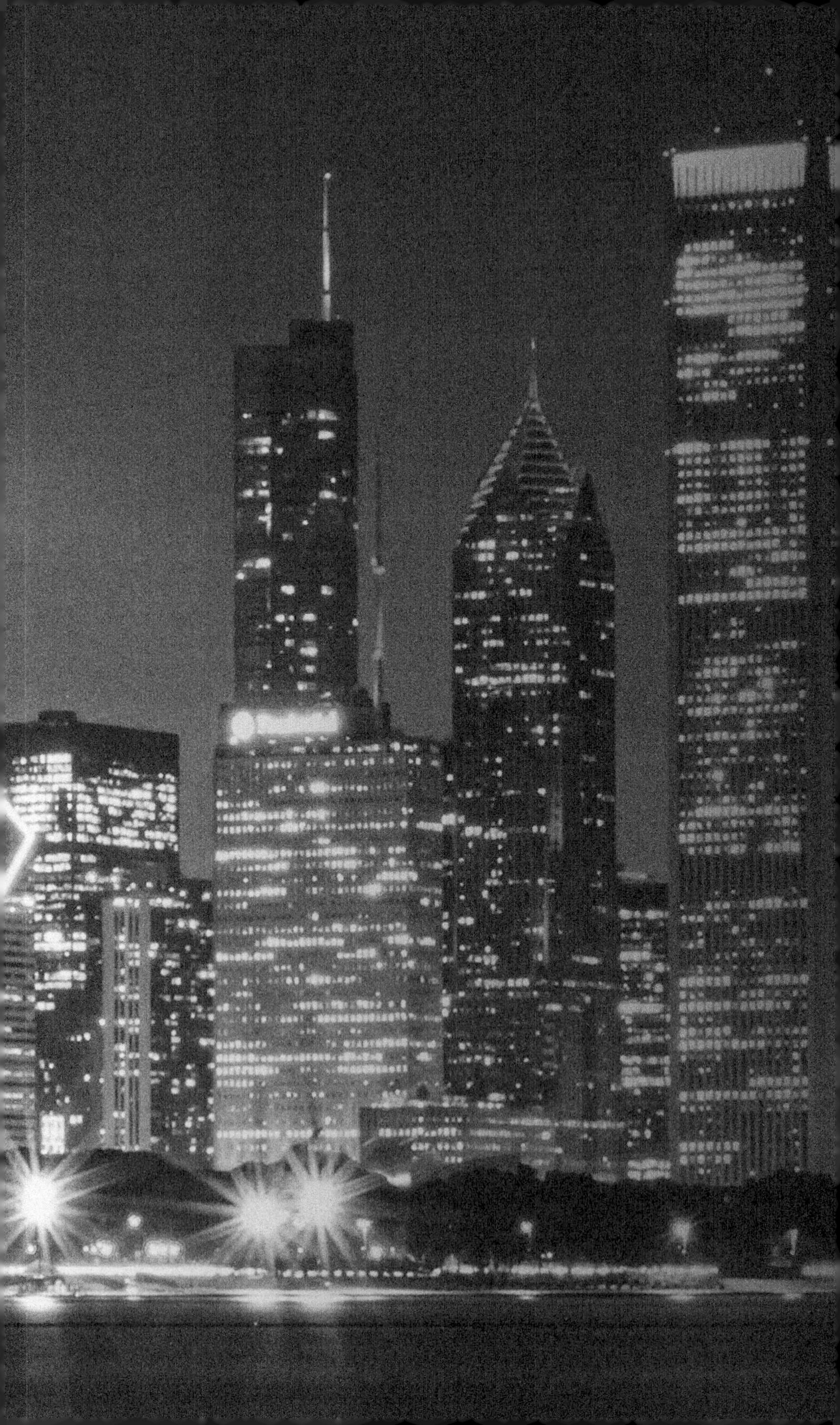

EPILOGUE

Alessio

"Uh oh. It looks like we need to wake up the princess," I whispered to my son.

"Wake Mama!" Christiano chanted, clapping his chubby hands from where we stood in the doorway.

Nivea was sprawled at an angle across the mattress, her hair an inky ocean spread over the tangled white bedding. I'd gotten in late last night and Christiano had been giving my wife hell. I'd taken over and made her go to bed. The little shit went right to sleep for me. It had been no chore to go join my wife in our room.

I brought him closer to the bed and sat him down. He crawled closer and got up on his knees. He leaned over her and carefully gave her a kiss. Okay, maybe not very carefully, because a long line of slobber followed as he pulled away. He was only two and tended to be a bit exuberant with his kisses.

"Wake up, Snow White. Your prince is here," I softly murmured.

Niv's thick, dark lashes fluttered, then she blinked a few

times to clear the dreams from her eyes. The corners of her mouth slowly lifted as she smiled sleepily up at our son.

"Good morning, handsome prince," she murmured to our dark-haired little boy. He quickly scooted under the covers with his mama.

"Give Mama another kiss, we need to get your shoes on. Nana and Poppa will be up to pick you up soon," I told him. They had called to say they were coming up the elevator.

"Mmmuahh!" He drew out the noise as he kissed her again.

"I'll get up so I can see Mom and Dad for a minute," she said with a yawn as she sat up in the bed. Her tousled waves fell around her shoulders in a beautiful disarray.

"No, they're staying for dinner when they bring him home later," I assured her.

"Oh, good," she happily sighed, then stretched as she yawned again.

"Stay here, I just wanted you to be able to say goodbye to our boy before he left," I explained, before I scooped Christiano up again. Niv's parents had moved to Chicago to be closer to their grandson. We had bought a home in Texas where we spent the winters so Christiano could be by my parents part of the year, too.

As I was walking out to answer the door, I snagged Christiano's backpack from where I'd placed it on the table.

Matt and Charlotte immediately reached for their grandson, and he practically flew into their arms. I had to hold him tight because he practically dove at them.

"There's my handsome grandson!" Charlotte cooed.

Yep, I was positive he was going to be spoiled rotten while he was gone.

"Dinner at six?" Matt clarified.

"Yep," I concurred.

"Perfect. Well, we'll get out of your hair so you can go practice making more grandbabies for us," Charlotte announced and my mouth fell open.

Matt cringed. "Jesus Char, I don't want to imagine that."

"Well, you enjoy the fruit of those labors," Charlotte shot back with a smirk.

"We're out! Let's go before my ears start bleeding," Matt whispered the last part conspiratorially to Christiano, who simply giggled.

They left and I locked the door. Then I made a beeline for my bed and the beautiful goddess awaiting me there.

When I entered the room, her pajama top was in the middle of the floor, her pants outside the bathroom door. The shower was on behind the closed door, so I stripped and quietly went through the door and smiled when I met my wife's bright blue gaze through the already steaming shower glass.

"Mr. De Luca, why are you naked?" She asked with a coy and playful batting of her eyes.

A primal growl rumbled from me as I stalked toward her and opened the door. Stepping into the spray, I didn't stop until I had her back to the wall. "Because I have an unquenchable need for my princess," I told her, my voice dropped lower than normal.

"Your princess? Baby, I'm your queen," she wickedly grinned and corrected me.

My hands cupped her ass and I groaned at the way her cheeks filled my hands. "I love this ass," I said as I squeezed it.

"Yeah?" she asked in a husky tone.

"Hell yeah," I clarified before I lifted her and she wrapped her legs around my hips. "But I really, really love this."

My cock lined up with her slick hole and I slid in. We both gasped and clung to the other as we reveled in the sensation of my shaft filling her tight pussy.

"My queen," I breathed as I withdrew and drove back in hard.

Her head fell back and her lips parted. "My king," she whispered as her nails dug into my shoulders.

Then I showed her how much I worshipped her with each wild thrust. By the time her hot cunt pulsed, and she squirted her release all over my balls, I was filling her with my cum.

As we clung to each other under the spray of the water, surrounded by the steam, I was never more thankful for any botched job as I was for the one that brought me to her.

ACKNOWLEDGEMENTS

If you made it this far, wow, thank you so much. Now it's confession time. This book almost didn't make it to your hands. For so many reasons, but mostly, Alessio just didn't want to cooperate. To the point where I lost interest in his story and I wanted to toss it to the side. Instead, I stuck with his stubborn ass and well… here we are. I hope he didn't disappoint.

Pam, Christie, and **Kristin,** my betas and friends, thank you for reading Alessio and telling me he didn't suck. LMAO. I appreciate the time you always take out of your day to read my words and give me feedback. I also want to thank you for the encouragement when I was ready to throw in the towel.

Shelby of Bookworm Edits and Creations, you are my hero. Thank you for stepping in to pick up my mess. Don't hate me for still not getting my commas right even after seven years. I'm trying. Okay, maybe that's a lie. I still put them where I think they should be. Sorry bout dat.

My family, you are my biggest cheerleaders and sometimes I can't believe how proud you are of me. Thank you for doing your best to tame my squirrel moments and keep me focused. I understand it a hard and essentially thankless job. Thank you for bragging about me and treating me like I'm famous.

Going back to **Christie**—yeah, I realized I wasn't done with you. LMAO. Part of the reason Alessio was so elusive is because he was happening during my trip to Melbourne,

Australia for RARE. Christie, during that trip, you were an absolute rock star. Not only did you open your home to two people you'd never met in person, you showed us around, fed us, helped me with my preorders, and worked tirelessly as my PA during both days of the signing. Then you shipped out books to readers after I left for me. Not to mention the pile of books I left there with you to "babysit." LOL. Without you, that trip wouldn't have happened. Thank you for everything, but mostly thank you for being an amazing friend.

Thanks again to **Clarise Tan** for another gorgeous cover for the De Luca boys. I can't tell you how much I love them!

Reggie, this image of Cody was perfect for Alessio! You captured my character behind your lens without even knowing it. I thank you, because your work helped to make this a phenomenal cover!

Stacey, thank you again for always making my pages beautiful! You have truly outdone yourself with this series! It might be my favorite paperback series to date. Here's to many more stunning creations in our future.

PSH, my main squeeze. Thank you for pimping my books everywhere you go, even though I know their creation steals so much of my time. Thank you for understanding that I often work best under pressure and letting me create—while reminding me I also need sleep. LOL. Love you bunches!

The ladies of **Kristine's Krazy Fangirls**, y'all are the best. You're the lovers of my books, the ones that I share my funny stories with, the ones who cheer me on when I'm struggling with a book I promised you, and I love you all to pieces! (((BIG HUGS)))! I can't thank you enough for your comments, your support, and your love of all things books. Come join us if you're not part of the group www.facebook.com/groups/kristineskrazyfangirls

Often, I try to spin the military into my books. This is for many reasons. Because of those reasons, my last, but never least, is a massive thank you to America's servicemen and women who protect our freedom on a daily basis. They do their duty, leaving their families for weeks, months, and years at a time, without asking for praise or thanks. I would also like to remind the readers that not all combat injuries are visible, nor do they heal easily. These silent, wicked injuries wreak havoc on their minds and hearts while we go about our days completely oblivious. Thank you all for your service.

OTHER BOOKS BY
KRISTINE ALLEN

Demented Sons MC Series - Iowa
Colton's Salvation
Mason's Resolution
Erik's Absolution
Kayde's Temptation
Snow's Addiction

Straight Wicked Series
Make Music With Me
Snare My Heart (where the De Lucas first come out to play!)
No Treble Allowed
String Me Up

Demented Sons MC Series - Texas
Lock and Load
Styx and Stones
Smoke and Mirrors
Jax and Jokers
Got Your Six (Formerly in Remember Ryan Anthology)

RBMC - Ankeny Iowa
Voodoo
Angel
A Very Venom Christmas
Chains
Haunting Ghost
Charming Phoenix
Sabre
Facet (Coming Soon!)

RBMC - Dallas Texas
Taming Raptor
Raptor's Revenge
Sparking Ares
Blade (Coming Soon!)

The Iced Series
Hooking
Tripping
Roughing
Holding
Fighting Love

Heels, Rhymes, & Nursery Crimes
Roses Are Red (RBMC connection)
Violets Are Blue (Coming Soon!)

Pinched and Cuffed Duet with M. Merin
The Weight of Honor
The Weight of Blood (by M. Merin)

La Famiglia De Luca
Part of the MMM Mayhem Makers Collaboration
Blood Lust
Blood Money
Blood Ties

ABOUT THE AUTHOR

Kristine Allen lives in beautiful Central Texas with her adoring husband. They have four brilliant, wacky, and wonderful children. She is surrounded by twenty-six acres, where her five horses, four dogs, and six cats run the place. She's a hockey addict and feeds that addiction with season tickets to the Texas Stars (who are in the Calder Cup playoffs this year!). Kristine realized her dream of becoming a contemporary romance author after years of reading books like they were going out of style and having her own stories running rampant through her head. She works as a night shift nurse, but in stolen moments, taps out ideas and storylines until they culminate in characters and plots that pull her readers in and keep them entranced for hours.

Reviews are the life blood of an indie author. If you enjoyed this story, please consider leaving a review on the sales channel of your choice, bookbub.com, goodreads.com, allauthor.com, or your favorite review platform, to share your experience with other interested readers. Thank you! <3

Follow Kristine on:

Facebook www.facebook.com/kristineallenauthor

Instagram www.instagram.com/_kristine_allen_

Twitter @KAllenAuthor

TikTok: www.tiktok.com/@kristineallenauthor

All Author www.kristineallen.allauthor.com

BookBub www.bookbub.com/authors/kristine-allen

Goodreads www.goodreads.com/kristineallenauthor

Webpage www.kristineallenauthor.com

Printed in Great Britain
by Amazon